BENE

This is the second volume of the memoirs of Eric Carstairs which I have edited for publication. The first volume, which I entitled *Journey to the Underground World*, told of Eric Carstairs and his friend, Professor Potter. Descending by helicopter into the crater of an extinct volcano in North Africa, where they entered the astounding, gigantic cavern world of Zanthodon beneath the sands of the Sahara.

There they encountered monsters and marvels almost beyond belief. For into this Underground World had slunk, from the dawn of time, survivors from the lost ages of the ancient past—not only the great dinosaurs of the Jurassic, but the cave bear and sabertooth tiger which perished in the Ice Age.

As well, there had filtered down into Zanthodon survivals of ancient man—hairy, bestial, hulking Neanderthal—tall, athletic Cro-Magnon—and even stranger peoples, as the present volume demonstrates.

The struggle for survival in the hostile jungles and steaming seas and volcanic mountains of Zanthodon is harsh and rigorous. But along the way, Eric and the Professor made friends: Darya, the beautiful young Princess of the Stone Age, and mighty, faithful Hurok of Kor; loyal young Jorn the Hunter and Tharn of Thandar himself, stalwart and magnificent monarch of his prehistoric tribe.

Also—being only human!—they made enemies: One-Eye, the brutal Neanderthal, Fumio, the traitorous renegade, and the cunning and mysterious Xask. You will meet all of these personages in the present book, friends and foes alike, together with new friends and enemies.

If you have an appetite for weird and curious marvels—a thirst for swashbuckling derring-do; if you enjoy a story that pits a lone adventurer against uncanny dangers—a tale of a princess in peril, and a hero to battle ruthless foes to rescue her—then come, join Eric Carstairs as he explores that weird world beneath the earth's crust, where lurk monsters and marvels strangely surviving from lost ages—*Zanthodon!*

—*LIN CARTER*

"A very impressive figure of a man was this jungle monarch."

ZANTHODON

Lin Carter

Illustrated by
Thomas Kidd

DAW BOOKS, INC.
DONALD A. WOLLHEIM, PUBLISHER

1633 Broadway, New York, N.Y. 10019

COPYRIGHT ©, 1980, BY LIN CARTER.

All Rights Reserved.

Cover art by Thomas Kidd.

FIRST PRINTING, JUNE 1980

1 2 3 4 5 6 7 8 9

DAWₛₖ
BOOKS

DAW TRADEMARK REGISTERED
U.S. PAT. OFF. MARCA
REGISTRADA. HECHO EN U.S.A.

PRINTED IN U.S.A.

CONTENTS

The World Beneath the World: A Foreword   i

I. THE LOST PRINCESS

1. Warriors of the Stone Age   11
2. The Parting of the Ways   17
3. Beyond the Peaks of Peril   24
4. Captive of the Corsairs   31
5. The Vampire Leech   37

II. THE PEAKS OF PERIL

6. Any Port in a Storm   47
7. The Door in the Cliff   53
8. An Unknown Enemy   61
9. Within the Mountains   68
10. The People of the Caverns   75

III. THE HOLLOW MOUNTAINS

11. The Things in the Pit   85
12. The Underground City   93
13. Warriors of Sothar   99

14. The Search for Darya   106
15. Stolen Moments   112

IV. THE FLIGHT FROM THE CAVERNS

16. When Rogues Flee   119
17. The Opening of the Door   126
18. Burning Bright   132
19. Pursued   139
20. Hidden Eyes   145

V. VICTORY IN ZANTHODON

21. The Bond of Friendship   153
22. Into the Caverns   159
23. Fumio Reappears   164
24. A Timely Interruption   171
25. The Dragonmen of Zar   179

The People of Zanthodon: An Afterword   186

LIST OF ILLUSTRATIONS

"A very impressive figure of a man was this jungle monarch." ii

"The unblinking gaze of those six staring eyes held the professor frozen." 39

"One-Eye came charging out of the edge of the woods." 59

"They went about their tasks like so many zombies." 97

"There seemed little the savage girl could do to fight her captors." 172

This book is for my friends
Joe and Dotty Schaumburger,
Frank and Carol Price, and
for the late Ken Beale.

Part One

THE LOST PRINCESS

Chapter 1.

WARRIORS OF THE STONE AGE

As somebody once said, without the power of sheer coincidence life would be duller than dishwater. Or if nobody ever said it, somebody *should* have.

It had been pure coincidence that I had met Professor Percival P. Potter, Ph.D., in the native bazaar of Port Said. If I had come along a moment or two earlier—or a moment or two later—we would never have encountered each other. And he would never have hired me and my Sikorsky helicopter, Babe, for his expedition into the Ahaggar region of North Africa.

Which would have meant that neither of us would have found our way into the Underground World of Zanthodon.

For beneath the hollow mountain, far below the earth's crust, we discovered a vast cavernous region presumably created by the impact of an enormous meteor of antimatter in prehistoric times. Whispered of in old Sumerian myths, Babylonian legends, Hebrew writings, the Underground World, we found, was a realm of marvels and perils beyond belief.

For into that gigantic subterranean land had filtered, over the ages, remnants of the extinct dinosaurs of the Jurassic and sabertooths and cave bears and mastodons from the Ice Age. And *men*, too—both the hulking, apelike and primitive Neanderthals and their tall, stalwart, handsome near-contemporaries, the Cro-Magnons, our own direct ancestors.

Locked together in a life-or-death struggle for survival were these twin branches of primordial humankind . . . and both were at war with hostile nature, the savage wilderness and the mighty beasts that roamed and ruled this fantastic world.

Into the very midst of that endless war for survival and su-

11

premacy the Professor and I had been thrust. Captured by slave raiders from the Neanderthal country of Kor, we had met and befriended the beautiful Stone Age girl, Darya, who had won us to the cause of her people.

She was about seventeen and absolutely the most gorgeous girl I have ever seen. Which may perhaps explain how she recruited so easily a tough, hard-bitten soldier of fortune like myself, and a wooly-headed, absentminded old scientist like Doc.

Not only was the Cro-Magnon girl the most beautiful thing I've ever laid eyes on, but she was also totally different from the women I had previously known. Nearly naked, save for a skimpy, apron-like garment of soft, elegantly tanned furs, which extended over one breast and shoulder but left bare the other perfect young breast and creamy, rounded shoulder, she was lithe and supple, her slim, tanned body graceful as an acrobat's. She had a long, flowing mane of silky hair the color of ripe corn and wide, dark-lashed eyes as blue as rain-washed April skies and a full, luscious mouth the tint of wild strawberries.

Darya had been a revelation to me: imagine a girl who had never heard of perfume, cosmetics, mascara or under-wired bras . . . a young female ignorant of the latest fads and fashions . . . a lithe, teen-aged Amazon who could swim, hunt, fight like a man but was as soft and sweet and demure as any princess in a fairy tale.

Such was Darya, *gomad* or princess of the Stone Age kingdom of Thandar. Is it any wonder I had fallen helplessly in love with her?

Together we had managed to escape from our captivity by the Apemen of Kor, but not without making some enemies. Among these foes were Fumio, the handsome but villainous Cro-Magnon chieftain who had been an unsuccessful suitor for Darya's hand; and One-Eye the Neanderthal, who had seized the kingship of Kor when I had slain Uruk the former High Chief with my revolver; and Xask, wily and cunning vizier of Kor, who was of neither race, but an exile fled from the wrath of his own mysterious people, who dwelt somewhere in the interior, far from the shores of the sea of Sogar-Jad.

But we had made good friends, as well. There was Hurok, the brawny Neanderthal to whom I had taught the meaning of friendship; and Jorn the Hunter, a brave youth from Darya's tribe; and her mighty sire himself, Tharn, stalwart Omad or king of distant Thandar.

Just when it seemed that all of our difficulties were at an end, the mysterious force of coincidence intervened once again.

Pursued by a great war party of Korians, Tharn's small host of warriors (searching for the lost Darya) had seemed outmatched. But a fortuitously timed stampede of huge pachyderms had crushed the Apemen of Kor, while the men of Thandar had fled to safety behind the dense wall of the jungles. We did not at that point in our adventures realize that Xask, One-Eye and Fumio had eluded the destruction which had consumed the warriors of Kor.

However, coincidence had separated us. Jorn the Hunter and Professor Potter had sought to penetrate a narrow pass through the Peaks of Peril, believing they were closely behind the long-lost Darya. What they in fact discovered beyond those sinister mountains we, far behind them, did not at that time know. Neither did we know that Jorn, that gallant and faithful youth, had seemingly perished not long thereafter—leaving the helpless old scientist alone and friendless in the most hostile wilderness on (or under) the earth.

I had been separated from my friends, remaining with Darya's mighty sire and his small force of fighting men, and with me was my giant friend, Hurok. At this time, I was ignorant of the fates which had befallen Jorn, Darya and the Professor, as were they of mine.

All I knew was that my friends were lost somewhere in the fetid jungles or grassy plains or unexplored mountains of Zanthodon. And in this weird and magnificent and terrible lost world ten thousand perils lie in wait for the unarmed or unwary traveler.

Even at this moment my beloved Darya might be suffering the cruelest of dooms.

Even now my friends might be staring into the fanged maw of one of the enormous predators that ruled this savage world.

And I—would I ever know of their end?

In the first section of these journals I have narrated the tale of our adventures up to this point in far more explicit detail than the brief, cursory account given above. Since I cannot be fully certain that the first part of my journal* has survived intact the rigors of travel, I have briefly encapsulated a description of how my friends and foes and I arrived at this point in our travels.

Now let me take up my tale where I left it off . . . for, if anything, the second part of my adventures in Zanthodon the Underground World is even more incredible and fantastic than that which I have previously narrated.

If any eye but mine will ever peruse these words, that is. . . .

Under the eternal noontide skies of Zanthodon we rested and broke our fast. Huntsmen easily found the woods teeming with game, for the stampede of the mammoths had driven smaller and more defenseless creatures from the plain to take refuge in the jungle's edge, even as we had done.

In no time, cook-fires flared along the margin of the jungle and the air was redolent with the aroma of roast uld turning slowly on the spit.

Squatting on our heels, our backs to the bole of a mighty Jurassic conifer, we consulted as to the course of action we should choose, the leaders of the Thandarian host and I.

Dominating the council, as he would naturally dominate any gathering into which he entered, was Tharn, Omad or King of the Stone Age realm of Thandar, which lay distantly somewhere to the south.*

A very impressive figure of a man was this jungle mon-

---

* Survive it did, and it came into my hands by curious means I am still not permitted to disclose. Suffice it to say, however, that the first volume of Eric Carstairs' account of his adventures in Zanthodon has been edited by myself and was recently published by DAW books under the title of *Journey to the Underground World*. Since I am unable to explain how the manuscript came into my possession, my publishers have chosen to regard this as purely a work of fiction, placing no credence in my claims that the story is presumably a true account, and it was published under the name of Lin Carter.

* Such directions are, of course, utterly meaningless in this subterranean world where the sun never shines. Lit forever by the perpetual phosphorescence of the cavern's roof, the Underground World and its denizens have no need for such referents. But I believe Eric Carstairs uses such terms as north, south, east and west in the manner of a convenient verbal shorthand. The Cro-Magnons had yet to invent the compass.

arch. Taller and heavier than I, his magnificent frame was superbly equipped with massive thews, and the innate majesty of his mien and manner would have marked him as royal in any age or society. His features were stern, with a strong jaw and fierce blue eyes under a lofty brow, framed in thick yellow mane and short curly beard. Heavy mustaches swept back to either side of his mouth and his head was crowned with a peculiar headdress whose main ornaments were two curved ivory fangs of prodigious length—the fangs of the vandar, or giant sabertooth. A triple necklace of the fangs of smaller beasts circled his strong throat. His tanned, muscular torso was bare, but there were heavy rings of bronze clasped about his brawny arms. An abbreviated garment of dappled fur clothed his loins, laced buskins of tanned leather clad his feet, a bronze dagger slept in its sheath of reptile hide at his waist, secured by a thong. Beside him, never far from his right hand, a long spear with leaf-shaped blade of hammered bronze rested against the tree trunk, and at his left a long wickerwork shield lay, covered with thick, tough hide.

Such a man was Tharn of Thandar, King of the Stone Age.

Just then he was speaking. The crude, primitive language spoken universally across the breadth of Zanthodon assumed dignity and resonance as it fell slowly from his lips.

"Against all hope, our enemies have been dispersed and trodden into the dust," he said solemnly. "This victory, while not entirely of our own devising, yet stands to be acted upon. Shall we next pursue what remnants of the Drugars survived the stampede of the herd of trantors, follow them to their distant country of Kor upon the island of Ganadol and thus exterminate their repellent kind from the world forever . . . or shall we search yet farther for the gomad Darya, my daughter, who may yet live? What say you?"

Komad pursed his thin lips judiciously. The grizzled old chief scout, who sat across from his lord, was lean and wiry as the shaft of a spear. He said little, leaving the talk to others more voluble than himself; but when such a man as Komad speaks, men tend to listen.

"We came into this country to find the Princess, my Chief," said Komad shortly. "It would be less than manly to give over that quest until we have proof that she no longer lives. As for the Drugars, they are few and scattered and can do us little harm, now or later. Let them slink back to Kor with their tails between their legs, unmolested."

The others grunted in agreement. Beside me, Hurok shifted his enormous bulk uncomfortably. The Drugars do not like to be called Drugars, any more than the panjani enjoy being called panjani. This seems to be the way of the world, as I have observed the same reaction among the peoples of the earth's surface as well.*

I turned to Hurok, questioningly.

"What is your opinion?" I asked him bluntly. "Do the Korians pose any further danger to us, or did the trantor stampede virtually wipe them out?" The question was not as rude as it may sound: outlawed by Uruk and hated by the present Chief, One-Eye, Hurok must from now on consider his own people to be his enemies.

He regarded me solemnly, shrewd, melancholy eyes blinking from beneath his overhanging brow.

"Few are the warriors of Kor left to give battle against Black Hair and his people," he grunted, Black Hair being Hurok's name for me. "No fewer than five tens of dugouts it must have taken to bring the warriors of Uruk the Chief hither, with no fewer than ten of the men of Kor in each. All, or almost all, must have been slain by the arrows of the Thandarians or beneath the feet of the trantors."

His heavy voice was somber as he recited the numbers of his tribe who had perished upon this very plain less than an hour ago. As well it might be, for five hundred warriors had died here . . . and, although cruel savages, the Apemen are brave and mighty warriors.

"And what say you, Eric Carstairs?" the jungle monarch inquired gravely. I shrugged.

"As for myself, I shall continue the search for Darya, your daughter, and for my friend Professor Potter, wherever you and your men choose to march," I said quietly.

A proud gleam shone approvingly in the eagle eyes of Tharn. He nodded with dignity.

"So be it, then," the High Chief said. "The search goes on."

---

* Drugars, in the universal language of Zanthodon, means "the Ugly Ones," and is used by the Cro-Magnons to refer to the Neanderthals. It may be presumed that, among themselves, the Drugars employ a more polite name for their own race. Panjani means "smoothskin" and is used by the Neanderthals to describe the Cro-Magnons, who doubtless also have another name for themselves.

Chapter 2.

THE PARTING OF THE WAYS

Tharn and his warriors—and Hurok and myself, as well—
were at that time suffering under a serious misapprehension.
For the evidence we had discovered in the glade seemed to
suggest that the Princess had been carried off and probably
devoured by one of the numerous gigantic predators who
roam this strange subterranean world.

This we believed for the simple reason that Tharn's scouts
had found the girl's tracks in a forest clearing, together with
certain articles which were thought to have belonged to
Darya of Thandar.

The footprints terminated in torn and blood-bespattered
turf, and while there were footprints leading to the spot, there
were none which led therefrom. . . .

But Tharn of Thandar was not completely convinced. To
such great-hearted men as the jungle monarch, death remains
unproven until the last doubt has been dissolved.

And as for myself, I could not believe that the gallant,
golden-haired girl was dead, that her bright, mercurial spirit
was forever quenched, and her slim, vibrant loveliness
mangled between the fearsome jaws of some mighty reptile
from Time's Dawn.

And, in actual fact, events had turned to other, happier
conclusions. For the fate of Darya was more mysterious and
far stranger than any of us could possibly have dreamed!

As you who have read the first part of these journals may
remember, the cave girl had actually been carried off by a
giant pterodactyl, but this occurred shortly after she had been
attacked and almost raped by Fumio, from whom Jorn rescued her. The marks of trampled turf found by the Thandarian scouts and huntsmen were the scene of her attack by

17

the villainous Fumio. We were at this time still ignorant of
the fact that the flying reptile had borne her far from this
place to its nest amid the Peaks of Peril to the north, beyond
the plains of the trantors.

Therefore—whether alive or dead—we all believed Darya
to be somewhere near at hand.

We feasted upon the roast uld and other game slain by the
huntsmen. Then we rested briefly from our battle against the
Apemen of Kor, while the warriors gathered up those of their
arrows which had not been broken beneath the trampling feet
of the stampeding mammoths, and their flung spears which
had likewise survived intact.

Soon we went forward along the edge of the jungle, with
search parties combing the depths of the woods while keen-
eyed scouts searched the plains for some sign of Darya, Jorn
and the Professor.

I strode along behind the others, feeling restless and ill at
ease. Everything within me instinctively hungered to strike
forth on my own to search for my lost friends. I have always
been a loner, never much of one for teamwork. And it
seemed to me, with half a hundred warriors, scouts and
hunters along, the weight of our numbers would somehow
slow me down in my personal quest.

I don't know quite how to explain this to you; it was just a
feeling in my bones that I would accomplish more, and more
swiftly, if I were on my own.

We were moving steadily west, toward the shores of the
Sogar-Jad, with the jungle at our left and the plains to our
right.

Beyond those plains loomed the peaks of mountains unknown to me. Glancing curiously at them, I thought to ask
Hurok what he knew concerning them.

"Men call them the Peaks of Peril," he said in his solemn,
deep voice. "Black Hair would be wise to avoid them, for
they have an unwholesome reputation. And Black Hair's she
could not possibly have gone so far."

"How do you know?" I demanded testily. "She could be
anywhere, by this time."

Hurok regarded me, a look of baffled uncomprehension in
his dim eyes. I have remarked before on the remarkable fact
that the warriors of Zanthodon are completely ignorant of the
existence of time, and have no word for the concept in their
language. I had, unthinkingly, employed the English word in

lieu of a Zanthodonian equivalent.* Hence, I had puzzled him.

We plodded along in the wake of the more swiftly moving Thandarians, who advanced along the margin of the jungle at a steady, space-devouring trot. I found myself lagging behind.

"Black Hair does not wish to accompany his people?" inquired Hurok after a time. I had explained to him that these were not my people, of course, and that my own homeland lay a vast distance away, but to the limited intelligence of the Apeman there were only two races of men—Drugars and panjani. And I was a panjani; hence Darya's people were my own.

I shook my head wordlessly, not bothering to answer, knowing I could not successfully put into words the vague feelings that oppressed my spirits. But I kept looking across the plains at the row of sharp-toothed mountains my companion had called the Peaks of Peril. Something about them attracted my restless, wandering attention. . . .

When Xask and Fumio had observed, from the safety of the great trees which stood like a palisade along the jungle's edge, the carnage which had destroyed all but a few of the Drugars when they were caught and trampled under the thundering feet of the stampeding pachyderms, they rightfully concluded that their continued presence in these parts could easily constitute a disaster; for, if Tharn and his warriors caught them lurking in the underbrush, both would have a heavy price to pay.

Xask was known as the renegade vizier who had formerly served Uruk, High Chief of the Apemen of Kor. And, as for Fumio, like all cowardly traitors, he was tormented by dread that his attempted rape of Tharn's daughter had been discovered by now. Neither of this pretty pair of villains wished to hang around long enough to be discovered, and neither desired to face the music.

So, after a mutual glance, they melted into the underbrush and vanished among the trees. True, neither could think of

---

* Remarkable, indeed, but doubtless natural enough, in a world devoid of day and night, whose climate remains eternal summer, without the cycle of the seasons or the grand wheeling of stars and constellations. The denizens of such a world would probably have no reason to invent so abstract a concept as that of time.

any particular haven of safety to which they could flee, but almost anywhere else in Zanthodon was healthier for them than where they were.

So eager were they to be gone that they did not stick around long enough to learn that One-Eye had cleverly escaped the doom of his countrymen. The cruel and brutal bully had survived the stampede by the merest chance, flinging himself prone in a narrow trench as the mammoths came thundering down upon the Apemen. Bruised and battered, covered with dirt and nearly deafened from the earth-shaking tread of the maddened pachyderms, he had nevertheless lived through the ordeal and was not seriously harmed. As soon as he could safely do so, One-Eye came scrambling up out of his hole in the ground and took to the trees.

With the agility of the apelike ancestors he so closely resembled, he quickly scaled one of the lofty Jurassic conifers. Lying flat upon a mighty branch, he searched the aisles of the jungle beneath his aerie with one squinting, keen eye. And thus it was that he observed the hasty and surreptitious flight of Xask and Fumio, both of whom he instantly recognized.

To be lost and alone in a jungle now swarming with his deadly enemies was not a situation which exactly appealed to the hulking Neanderthal. Without thought, almost by instinct alone, he sprang from the branch, seizing a long jungle vine, and swung into the upper branches of a neighboring tree. Traveling in this manner, he was able to outdistance the Thandarians, and to keep his two erstwhile confederates in view.

For a plan was slowly evolving through the dim, dull wits of One-Eye.

And unfortunately it involved myself!

It was not long before Xask and Fumio discovered that they were being pursued.

Seizing the slight arm of his comrade, Fumio uttered a warning word. Then, dropping prone upon the ground, the Thandarian warrior pressed one ear against the turf. Far and faint the sounds of running feet were, but a hunter of the Stone Age develops keen senses or starves.

He raised a frightened face to Xask. "They are following us!" whimpered Fumio. His companion regarded him quizzically.

"*Who* is following us?" he inquired curiously.

"It can only be Tharn—Tharn the Mighty!" cried Fumio in an agony of despair.

"Tharn, whose daughter you attempted to rape, before Jorn the Hunter made you turn tail and run?" inquired the other, maliciously.

The eyes of Fumio faltered and fell. "Even so," he breathed.

Xask regarded him thoughtfully. A tall and strikingly handsome specimen of manhood was Fumio of Thandar, but nature had made his heart weak and cowardly, and Jorn's fist had demolished his slim, handsome nose. Now, pale and sweating with fear, his sleek mane rumpled, his hands shaking, he was a remarkably unattractive specimen. And, for a moment, Xask considered deserting him and escaping alone, for he was becoming more of a liability than an asset.

But then he reconsidered. So far as Xask knew, the warriors and huntsmen of Thandar as yet had not learned of Fumio's traitorous attempt on the maidenhood of his princess. Thus they could hardly have reason to pursue the fugitives; doubtless, they were merely searching the jungles, hoping to find some trace of the lost girl.

In rapid words he apprised Fumio that his fears were groundless. Although relieved, Fumio was still worried.

"Perhaps so," he panted, "but if they continue in this direction, they will find us, nonetheless. . . ."

"Then we will climb a tree," suggested Xask. "And they will go by underneath us. Since they are not searching for us, they will not bother searching the treetops to find us. Come—let us do this quickly. I have no wish to be taken prisoner by the enemies of Kor, for many of them will know of my former position among the Drugars."

Fumio possessed great strength and vigor, nor was Xask, with his slender, wiry build, exactly feeble. They ascended the nearest tree and found places to conceal themselves behind convenient masses of dense foliage.

Before long, the two observed a grizzled Thandarian enter their vicinity. Fumio easily recognized the man as Komad, leader of the scouts. They watched as he went past their airy perch without once pausing to search the foliage aloft with his keen eyes. He vanished into the jungle gloom, soon followed by others.

Once the main body of the Thandarian war party had passed them by, both fugitives breathed easier.

But not for very long. With startling suddenness, a massive

weight descended upon the broad branch where they crouched and huge hairy hands caught both men by the scruff of the neck, knocking their heads together with a resounding thump.

Dizzy—fear-frozen—they stared up into the ugly, grinning visage of One-Eye!

Displaying broken, discolored, tusk-like teeth in a broad grin, their captor uttered a phlegmy grunt, which was obviously his version of amused laughter.

"One-Eye never knew before that snakes could climb trees!" he chuckled.

Hurok surveyed me puzzledly, for the two of us had fallen well behind the main body of the Thandarians and I must have seemed to my giant friend reluctant, for some mysterious reason, to keep up with them.

"If Black Hair lingers here, his people will outdistance him," he observed at last.

I nodded, saying nothing. The fact of the matter was, quite simply, something within me clamored urgently to know about that row of distant rocky spires the savages knew by the ominous name of the Peaks of Peril.

A silent inward voice seemed to be drawing my attention thither. And I could not explain this to my huge companion any more than I could explain it to myself. But a lifetime of adventure and danger had taught me to trust my intuition.

And intuition told me I should strike forth on my own and venture among the Peaks of Peril.

I had, at that time, no way of knowing that it was into the shadow of those mysterious mountains that Darya, my beloved, had vanished. Instinct alone urged me thither.

But to leave the safety afforded by numbers and to venture forth on my own was more than reckless, it was downright foolhardy. And I certainly had no right to risk the life of my faithful, loyal friend Hurok in following a mere hunch.

"I have decided not to accompany the *panjani*," I explained haltingly to my companion. "Something calls me to those peaks, and I must follow that call. . . ."

He regarded me with curiosity in his small, dim eyes.

"Is it that Black Hair feels his stolen she might be found in the mountain country?" he asked after a small lapse of time in his heavy bass voice. I shrugged helplessly.

"I do not know!" I confessed.

He regarded me stolidly, his expression unreadable.

After a time, he grunted, "To quit the war party of the *panjani* and go forth into an unknown country is very dangerous." It was a remark made in neutral tones, not a complaint or an argument.

"I know," I said. "And I will not ask you to go with me, Hurok, my friend. The *panjani* will not harm you, for they know you to be my friend. You need not accompany Black Hair into the unknown—for those peaks, you have told me, have a most unsavory reputation. Let me go on my own way and follow where my heart urges me; you can always go back to Kor and rejoin your own people. With Uruk and One-Eye dead, you could become the High Chief yourself! It would be very selfish of me to try to hold you by my side when you have no longer any reason to journey with me."

He regarded me with a somber gaze.

"Is it that Black Hair no longer wishes the company of Hurok?" he inquired at last.

I opened my mouth to deny that assumption. Then I closed it, saying nothing. Perhaps the most gentlemanly thing for me to do was to permit him to think I no longer wished his companionship, although that was certainly untrue. But to urge him to go with me into danger for my own selfish purposes was unfair. Guiltily, I decided to evade the question.

"You may think what you wish," I said coolly.

He gave me one long, searching look. Then, without a word or gesture of farewell, he turned on his heel and vanished into the underbrush.

I sighed, feeling a pang of dismay and loss go through my heart. But it did seem, at the time, the only thing to do.

Nevertheless, I had a feeling that I had just made one of the worst mistakes in my life. . . .

I turned away and struck out across the plains, heading for the shadowy peaks to which my heart called me.

And behind me in the treetops, three cold and cunning pairs of eyes gleamed with unholy joy as my giant companion deserted me and I went forth alone and friendless into the Unknown.

Chapter 3.

BEYOND THE PEAKS OF PERIL

At this time only one person knew the truth of Darya's whereabouts and the mystery of her predicament, and that person was my old friend Professor Percival P. Potter, Ph.D.

Since the Professor and I first penetrated the earth's crust and discovered this forgotten land of Zanthodon, we had been constant companions. Together we had descended down the hollow shaft of the inactive volcano. Together we had been captured by the Apemen of Kor, making the acquaintance of Darya, Fumio and Jorn the Hunter, who had been among our fellow captives. Together we had shared many exciting adventures and had faced shoulder to shoulder many perils.

But events had sundered our paths, and each of us had gone our own way.

Jorn the Hunter, that brave young cave boy, and the Professor had followed in the direction the pterodactyl had flown when it had carried off Darya from the jungle clearing. It had borne its helpless burden beyond the jungle's edge and across the grassy plains to its nest high among the Peaks of Peril. And thither had Jorn and Professor Potter journeyed, hoping to rescue the girl.

But other dangers were to come, and from the very last of these she was not to effect an escape. For Jorn and the Professor had found a path through the Peaks, emerging to find on the other side a spectacle as inexplicable as it was amazing.

Having managed to escape from the nest of the pterodactyl, descending from the heights to the beach beyond the mountains, Darya had been enjoying a refreshing bath in the river when an unseen watcher surprised her.

And what Jorn and the Professor observed when they pen-

24

etrated at last to the far side of the Peaks of Peril was a scene fantastic, terrifying and incredible!

Naked and struggling in the brawny arms of her villainous and swarthy turbaned captors, the Princess was about to be forced aboard an astonishing vessel. It was *a full-rigged galley* of Moorish or perhaps Saracenic design, with a green banner fluttering from its masthead, charged with the star and crescent of Muhammad the Prophet of Islam.

Such ships have not sailed the seas of the Upper World for generations—but here one was, and the Professor could only gape incredulously at the sight.

While Jorn stared with grim alarm, the Professor, shaken to the core of his being with sheer amazement, uttered a dazed ejaculation. From his omnivorous reading and the broad range of his scientific studies, he was able to recognize the sailing vessel and the dark-hued, bearded sailors as none other than mysteriously surviving descendants of the notorious Barbary pirates who had made all of the Mediterranean their realm until crushed by European troops in the early nineteenth century. They had since scattered, vanishing from the pages of history.

But what were Barbary pirates doing here in Zanthodon?

There could not yet be a simple answer to that mystery. But the enormity of the Underground World had already afforded a haven of safe refuge to many doomed denizens of past ages, from the dinosaurs and pterodactyls of the dim Jurassic to the Neanderthals, Cro-Magnons and giant sabertooth tigers of the Ice Age. Perhaps a handful of Barbary pirates, fleeing inland to avoid capture by the victorious Europeans, had made their way into Zanthodon, as well.

Such seemed to be the case, obviously.

While Professor Potter mused in his absentminded, scholarly way over the mystery, the simpler wits of Jorn grasped the girl's danger, and acted upon it instantly. Flinging his lithe young body into the seething waves of the Sogar-Jad, he swam to the galley's side in a gallant but hopeless attempt to save his Princess.

And then the villainous commander raised one bejeweled hand in a languid gesture, and archers cut the youth down even as he reached the galley's side. He sank without a trace and, as the Professor watched dazedly, numb with horror, the laughing pirate commander bore the nude body of the struggling Darya within his cabin and the ship got underway, cruising into the north, soon to vanish into the distance.

In reaction the old scientist fainted dead away there on the sandy shores of the underground sea. And, for a time, he knew no more.

When Professor Potter awoke from his swoon, his first instinct was to peer aloft into the misty skies of Zanthodon, thereby to ascertain the approximate hour of day from a perusal of the position of the sun. But there is, of course, no sun that illuminates the cavernous dome of the Underground World; vexed, the old man bit his lip and uttered a rude expletive.

He might have lain unconscious for many hours—or for only a few seconds. There was, quite simply, no way to tell. But, searching the billowy expanse of the Sogar-Jad, he saw no sign of the swarthy and beturbaned mariners who had carried off the Stone Age girl, nor any sign of their astoundingly antique vessel.

"Eternal Einstein!" said the Professor querulously. "The galley might be mere yards around the curve of the coast, or it could have sailed for leagues—and I have no way of telling which!"

Now, Percival P. Potter, Ph.D., was small and scrawny and elderly, certainly no young and vigorous fighting man. But the spark of old-fashioned chivalry that burns within the breasts of good and decent men blazed high within his gallant heart; and, man of action or no man of action, it went against the grain of such as Professor Potter merely to turn his back on Darya's frightening predicament and seek to return to the safety of his friends.

So he began to explore the curve of the coastline to make certain whether or not the galley was still in view. At this particular point, the shores of the Sogar-Jad protruded in a long promontory which, like a sheltering arm, protected the small lagoon in which the Barbary pirates had moored their craft. In order to gain a full and unimpeded view of the sea itself, the Professor would have to traverse this promontory to its farther side. And without a moment's hesitation, he proceeded to do so.

Thick tropical vegetation clothed the length of the narrow peninsula, down whose length marched like a rocky spine an extension of the Peaks of Peril, through which the Professor had but recently passed with Jorn.

And the moment this heavy wall of jungle closed about the old man, shutting from his view the warm light of open day, a peculiar premonition chilled his heart. There was nothing to meet the eye that hinted of concealed danger, and not the slightest sound reached the keen ears of the Professor, for all of the jungle drowsed in the simmering warmth of Zanthodon's eternal noon. But the senses of men, even civilized men, number more than the known and recognized five; some faint instinct of self-preservation roused within the breast of Professor Potter, alerting him to the fact that all was not well in this jungle.

Globules of cold perspiration burst forth upon his bald and bony brows, and a clamminess was in his sweating palms, while his brave old heart beat lightly but swiftly. Again and again, the savant wished mightily that I, Eric Carstairs, could have been at his side. For not only was I younger and stronger than he, and used to extricating myself from dangerous predicaments by brawn or brains or luck—but I still bore at my side the precious automatic pistol wherewith I had slain the brutal Uruk.

And the pistol, of course, was the only such weapon of its kind in all of the Underground World. How much more secure would the old man have felt, with me—and the gun— near to hand!

A dozen times within the first several minutes of sensing the presence of lurking danger the Professor stopped short, peering about into the motionless underbrush, straining every sense to search out the cause of his trepidations.

But nothing that he could see or hear or smell seemed to afford him the slightest danger. Skyward soared the massive boles of Jurassic conifers, and the gloom between their trunks was impenetrable and ominous. Silence reigned within the depths of the jungle, as if all nature held its breath in suspense, waiting for some secret signal.

Erelong, the Professor had reached the range of rocky hills that ran the length of this peninsula. For the jungle aisle he followed terminated abruptly and he found himself confronted by a sheer, unbroken wall of solid stone.

Pausing momentarily, the Professor considered which way to turn. It did not seem to be within the physical powers of the old man to scale this cliff-like wall of smooth gray rock, and he debated the relative wisdom of turning back along the way that he had come, to seek a side path or alternative route.

But to venture again into the depths of the jungle . . . not knowing what hideous monstrosity surviving from Time's forgotten dawn might be creeping on his track . . . that was almost more than the old man dared attempt.

Pondering this dilemma and striving to make up his mind what to do, the Professor stood there, brows knit, tugging thoughtfully and indecisively on his little wisp of stiff white goat-like beard.

And at that moment something moved behind him in the darkness.

He heard the snapping of a twig—

Startling loud in the ominous and all-pervading silence was that sudden sound—like a gunshot.

He whirled about, eyes starting from his head, mouth gaping open to give voice to a startled cry—

Then he froze—petrified with astonishment.

Could the Professor have somehow known that I was not very far distant from him, was, even at that very instant, traversing with all such speed as I was able to attain the broad and grassy plain of the trantors, the knowledge may well have comforted him in his present danger.

When Hurok had parted from me, driven away by the seeming coldness of my ungracious rebuff, I hastened to divert from my former path at right angles.

Ahead of me, Tharn and his troop of warriors were scouring the edges of the jungle, searching for any slightest sign or token that might denote the whereabouts of the missing princess. During the brief while that Hurok and I had lingered behind to discuss my vague premonitions, they had drawn quite a ways ahead of our position.

I then traveled rapidly out into the midst of the plain, taking for my goal the line of soaring gray mountains that were known as the Peaks of Peril. I was young and vigorous and had rested well after my recent exertions; hence it was that I had reached midway into the plain of the trantors at the precise moment that Professor Potter glimpsed with amazement his peril.

The exigencies of narrative technique require me, thus tiresomely, to relate matters of which, at the time, I had no actual knowledge in simultaneity with those events which I witnessed or partook in. That this must seem confusing to my reader—if any!—is regrettable, but necessary. It is, of course, only in retrospect, long after we had all come back again together and found sufficient leisure to relate the tale of our adventures to each other, that I was able to get straight in my mind what each of my friends or enemies was doing at any given point in time.

And now, long after these events transpired, I am able to narrate these adventures, diligently striving to explain what each of us was doing more or less at the same time. This requires me to cut back and forth from the viewpoint of one person to that of another, but I am no seasoned writer and know of no other way to set all of these things before you. Bear with me, then, as my narrative becomes even more confusing and complex with the diversity of incidents yet to come.

At the time, I had no way of knowing that I was being followed by anyone.

The wind was blowing into my face, all sound was dulled by the sighing of the long grasses and the thudding of my feet as I loped across the plain of the trantors, and I had no occasion to turn and look behind me.

After an interminable time I reached that mighty wall of gray and somber mountains that was my goal. Another hour or so of searching along the flanks of the mountain led me to the fortuitous discovery of a narrow ravine or chasm, into which I plunged. I followed the narrow way between the mountains as it twisted and turned, wearying now and beginning to become hungry.

And all the time, those that pursued me continued on my trail.

Before very much longer, I had penetrated the Peaks of Peril and had emerged on the far side of the range of mountains, to view a broad vista of shoreline and sea. Whether or not this was the same pass through the mountains which Jorn and the Professor had earlier followed I have no way of telling.

I was tired and hungry by this time, and, like an old campaigner, knew that I must pause, however briefly, to rest and to eat in order to take up again my quest with undiminished vigor.

No game presented itself, but the tidal pools along the shoreline contained a quantity of small fish marooned by the withdrawing of the tide. I made a fire with dry leaves and sticks, speared the three fish I had scooped out of the shallows with my bare hands, and cooked them over the sizzling flames.

Half-raw, half-burnt, the meat of the fish tasted to me

more delicious than the sumptuous dishes I had once sampled in the finest restaurants of Paris or Rome. Satisfying my thirst with cool, clear water from the little freshwater stream that meandered down the shore to empty into the sea, I made a nest for myself in the thick grasses and composed myself for slumber. I had intended a brief catnap to revitalize my strength, but now in retrospect, I fear that I fell into heavier slumbers than had been my intention.

And from my sleep I was awakened suddenly and rudely.

For One-Eye was kneeling upon my chest. And he had snatched the precious revolver from my waist and was at that moment pointing it into my face, with an evil lopsided grin.

Chapter 4.

CAPTIVE OF THE CORSAIRS

No words of mine can possibly do justice to the emotions which raged within the heart of Darya of Thandar. When the bearded chieftain of the corsairs had surprised her in the act of bathing in the little jungle stream, she had been furious and frightened. Helpless in the powerful embrace of the swarthy pirate, the girl had not been able to resist as he bore her aboard the Moorish galley and into his cabin.

Now, the Stone Age girl had, of course, never seen such a vessel as this, or such men as these in all her brief span of existence. Nor would the very name of the Barbary pirates have signified aught to the Cro-Magnon Princess. But to be plucked from the relative security of freedom and thrust into the captivity of hard and dangerous men is an experience disheartening and terrifying.

Hence, it is no reflection upon the brave and gallant spirit of the beautiful cave girl to admit that her heart faltered within her as she was borne, naked and struggling, within the cabin of the corsair chief.

With one booted foot the corsair kicked shut the door behind him. The furiously struggling girl he dumped unceremoniously onto his bed, a narrow bunk built into the curving hull of the pirate vessel. Then he stood grinning down at her as she lay, panting and disheveled and completely at his mercy.

For her part, Darya of Thandar took in the tall, commanding form of her captor with rage and detestation and a very natural amount of fear. Also very natural to the cave girl was the intense curiosity she felt as she examined with puzzlement the man who had seized her.

He was tall and hawk-faced, his lean, strong jaw adorned by a crisp trim of beard which was either naturally red in coloration or dyed to that hue. With the exception of the hulking Drugars, whose brawny, apelike forms were adorned by a short pelt of dirty russet fur, Darya had never before seen a man with red hair.

Nor a man so strangely clothed. For the pirate chieftain wore an old-fashioned corselet of overlapping bronze scales, a loose robe-like surcoat of coarsely woven cloth and a scarlet turban of rich silk bound about his brows. Jeweled rings adorned his fingers, a girdle of embossed leather cinched in his waist, boots of scarlet leather with toes that curled up were upon his feet.

The scent of perfume wafted from the folds of his raiment. A slender scimitar of cold steel was thrust through a loop fastened to his girdle; it slapped against his thigh as he moved. He was, all in all, the most curious figure of a man whom the maid had ever set eyes upon.

The information would have meant nothing at all to the girl, but the corsair was, of course, one of the modern descendants of the Barbary pirates who had been the merciless scourge of the Mediterranean many generations in the past.

And the man who now towered over her, tasting her nude loveliness with gloating black eyes, was none other than Kâiradine Redbeard, called Barbarossa—the seventh of his line to bear that once-feared and very famous name, as he was the seventh in direct succession from the notorious Khair ud-Din, pirate king of Algiers and last master of the Barbary corsairs.

And *this* was the man who had captured her!

The reason the Stone Age maiden had never before seen one of the Barbary pirates, nor even one of the high-prowed, red-sailed galleys of Moorish design which they continued to build in imitation of their piratical ancestors, was that the kingdom of Kâiradine Redbeard lay far to the "north" of this part of Zanthodon. Farther up around the curve of the coastline of the Sogar-Jad lay the stone-walled fortress citadel the pirates called El-Cazar.

And while they lived according to the custom of their ferocious ancestors—which is to say by preying upon the tribes and nations of the coast and of those islands upon the breast of the Sogar-Jad which were inhabited by men, or by creatures very much like men—never had the galleys of El-Cazar penetrated far enough into the southern parts of the underground ocean to loot or raid or plunder Darya's distant homeland, the kingdom of Thandar.

But while the figure and clothing of the Barbary corsair might be strange and unfamiliar to such as Darya, Kâiradine Redbeard had seen many Cro-Magnons of Darya's kind. For the blond and blue-eyed race of half-savage cavemen were closely akin to many scattered tribes and war clans throughout the Underground World.

Never before, however, had Redbeard laid his dark eyes upon so tempting a morsel of femininity as was Darya of Thandar.

She was indeed an exquisite creature, as she lay there on the bunk glaring up at him with fury and loathing mingled in her wide blue eyes. As she panted for breath, her perfect breasts rose and fell, their delectable pink tips crisped from the coldness of the sea air on her damp skin. The corsair let his eyes travel caressingly down the sleek curve of arm and shoulder, belly and flank and long, slim, tanned thigh.

"By the Veiled Prophet of Khorassan, wench, but you are a beauty!" the corsair breathed hoarsely as he reached out to fondle the nude and tempting loveliness sprawled out before him on the rumpled bedclothes.

Then, in the next instant, with a startled cry, he withdrew his hand, nursing it to his corseleted breast. For the girl had struck like an angry viper, sinking her strong teeth almost to the bone into the flesh of his hand. With a harsh oath, he stared at the red blood running down to drip from his fingertips, and raised his other hand to deal the savage girl a heavy blow.

But at that moment there occurred what could only be termed a fortuitous interruption.

To the rear of the corsair's cabin, which fronted upon the foam that boiled in the ship's wake, were a broad, curved row of diamond-paned windows.

These swung open suddenly as there came hurtling into the room a bronzed and naked figure, with wet, flying hair whipping about brawny young shoulders. And through this hair glared cold blue eyes, lion-like in their wrath.

As the consair gaped incredulously, his hand hovering for one indecisive moment above the hilt of his long, curved scimitar—that lithe and naked figure launched itself upon him like a human thunderbolt.

As for Darya of Thandar, the cave girl crouched amid the disordered tangle of the bedclothes, frozen with astonishment.

For the half-naked figure that had burst upon them so suddenly, with his unannounced and unanticipated but nonetheless extremely welcome and timely interruption, was one that she instantly recognized.

And, recognizing him, her blue eyes widened with sheer amazement.

For her intrepid rescuer was a man whom the girl knew very well to be dead.

For one long, frozen moment I stared up into the cold black eye of the unwavering gun muzzle. Then I sprang to my feet, hurling One-Eye onto his back with a thump that drew a growling oath.

And faced the three of them.

Fumio I already knew and disliked, for he was a treacherous coward and a preening swine.

Xask I had never seen before, and took in with one searching, curious glance. Slim of build, indeterminate of age, olive-hued, he resembled neither the russet-furred Apemen of Kor nor the stalwart blond savages of Darya's tribe. His eyes were cold and shrewd and black as ink, and his hair was sleek and neatly trimmed and black as well. But it was his garments that caught and held my stare, for they were of fine, woven cloth—here in this primitive wilderness, where all others save for the Professor and myself went half naked, clad only in tanned hide and furs!

One-Eye sprang to his feet, red murder burning in his little pig-like eye. Spitting curses, he came toward me, swinging his heavy, ape-like arms, the pistol forgotten in the grip of one huge hand.

But the one whom I soon came to know as Xask stayed him. The slender little man laid a thin hand on the Apeman's shaggy arm and murmured a word or two in his eye ear. Growling and licking his thick lips, One-Eye subsided.

I viewed the three of them with contempt.

"Well, here's a fine trio of rogues!" I said boldly, deciding that it was best under the circumstances to put a bold front on it before the world. "One-Eye, you'd better put down—and carefully—that piece of iron you thieved from my person, before it explodes and rips your arm off as it split asunder the villainous brain of Uruk, your Chief," I advised.

Beneath the dirt and matted fur that coated his ugly hide, One-Eye paled suddenly, staring down at the thing he held. And almost had he flung the pistol at my feet, as I had hardly dared hope he would. But Xask again stayed him with a crisp word.

"This *is* the famous thunder-weapon, then," murmured the wily former vizier of Kor. "We have heard much about it. Give it to me, One-Eye."

Not without reluctance, the hulking Neanderthal passed my pistol into the slim hands of the little man in the silken tunic. Xask handled it with cautious respect, turning it over and over in his hands.

"The workmanship is superb," he breathed at last, "and far beyond the abilities of the artisans of my people. Your tribe, Eric Carstairs, must be far advanced in the arts of civilization. You must teach me how to work the device."

I folded my bare arms across my chest and gave him a cool, level look.

"I'd rather deliver a box of dynamite to a murderous maniac than teach you how to use it," I said contemptuously.

A small smile hovered briefly about his thin lips.

"Well, as to that, we shall soon see. One-Eye has few virtues, but he is remarkably strong, and among his primitive kind, sheer cruelty is a trait necessary for survival. If it comes down to that, I believe a few minutes alone and helpless and in the grip of those huge paws will have you screaming for the opportunity to teach me how to use the weapon," Xask said cleverly. And One-Eye leered and balled one huge fist suggestively.

I gave Xask stare for stare, and did not permit the slightest flicker of expression to mar my mask of nonchalant and contemptuous ease. But I could well imagine the brutalities of which the savage Neanderthal was fully capable, and my heart sank within me, wondering how much suffering I could endure in his grip before my will crumbled and my resolve broke.

It is not an easy question for any man to have to ask himself. And while I am, perhaps, bolder and stronger than most, and have lived a desperate life crowded with danger, the thought of torture touches the secret craven hidden in every man.

I did not care to have to put my own courage to *that* test.

"But," smiled Xask with an easy shrug, "for the moment I am weary and also hungry. Fumio, bind our prisoner and see to it that he cannot wriggle free. One-Eye, come and help me build up the fire again . . . for I perceive that our friend did not entirely finish his fish dinner, and it has been long since I myself dined."

They bound me, Fumio twisting my hands behind my back with cruel, numbing strength, and left me propped against a boulder while they rested at their ease, basking before the fire, leisurely finishing my meal for me.

And all the while, Xask eyed the automatic with shrewd, thoughtful, clever eyes.

Chapter 5.

THE VAMPIRE LEECH

When Professor Percival P. Potter, Ph.D., saw the thing that came slithering out of the shadows of the jungle, three things occurred almost simultaneously.

He paled to the color of fresh milk; his heart sank into what remained of his waterlogged boots and remained there, feebly palpitating; and his scientific curiosity awoke within him to acute and fascinated intensity.

During the weeks that he had spent here in the Underground World, the Professor had seen a wide assortment of rare and remarkable survivals from the remote eons of Earth's distant past.

The omodon, or great Cave Bear of the Ice Age, and its contemporaries, the wooly mammoth which the men of Zanthodon call the thantor and the dreaded sabertooth tiger, the vandar. As well, he had viewed with awe and amazement survivals from the Age of Reptiles, such as the grymp, or triceratops, the plesiosaur, which the primitives call the yith, and that fantastic flying dragon of the dawn, the mighty pterodactyl—the thakdol, as the men of the Underground World term it.

But the elderly savant had also observed species hitherto unknown to men of science and as yet unrecorded in their fossil histories, and had heard of yet others unfamiliar to him and probably unknown—such as the enormous albino spiders called the vathrib, and a kind of giant serpent, the xunth, which attains a length of more than thirty feet.

The creature which now came creeping upon him out of the underbrush was like nothing which Professor Potter had ever seen or heard of before.

It was a huge, slimy, crawling slug or leech, and it was nearly *five feet* in length. The curved back of the creature

37

was in color a slick, leathery brown, but its under-surface was
tender pink in hue.

That tender and fleshy underbelly was lined with hard
suckers, like craters left by a broken pustule. The Professor
shuddered in loathing at the thought of those suckers clasping
naked human flesh, and sucking therefrom the hot blood of
men, as do the smaller leeches of the Upper World.

But the most horrible and repellent feature about the monstrous leech was not its size or its nature, but the uncanny
gleam of cold, inhuman *intelligence* that burned in its eyes.

For the front portion of the enormous slug-like thing ta-
pered into something like a curled snout. This obscene proboscis—it could hardly be dignified by calling it a
head—bore rows of small, gleaming red eyes. These were six
in all. And within them glowed an alien sentience that was
appalling: they possessed at once the chill, unwinking fascination of the eyes of a cobra . . . and an intellect vast,
frigid, awesome.

The unblinking gaze of those six staring eyes held the old
man frozen where he stood, as the gaze of a serpent re-
putedly is able to root to the spot the helpless fowl which is
to be its prey.

Dizzily, the Professor stared into that febrile, unwavering
and multiple glare. In his fear-frozen mind, it seemed that the
six eyes expanded like unto mad red moons, until staring into
them was like staring into the lambent but motionless depths
of a sea of scarlet luminance.

And all the while that it held the old man rooted to the
spot with its unwinking and hypnotic stare, the monstrous
leech-like thing crept slowly nearer and nearer to where he
stood.

Sick with fear, petrified with fascination, the Professor
dimly guessed that the gigantic leech lived upon the blood of
men and of beasts, much as do the smaller leeches he was
familiar with in the world above. They are noisome and
squeamish-making, but due to their smallness, can do a full-
grown man little harm.

But the leech that slithered and crept toward him now was
nearly as tall as he was.

And the horrible mouths of those crater-like excrescences
that lined its pink and tender underbelly could suck a man
dry in minutes.

There was nothing the old man could do to defend himself
against the slimy vampire leech. Fast fixed in the hypnotic

"The unblinking gaze of those six staring
eyes held the professor frozen."

gaze of those snakelike eyes, he was utterly unable to move
so much as the tip of one finger. And even if he had been
able to move, his back was set against a sheer wall of unbroken stone, and the only aisle through the dense, thick wall of
solid vegetation was the aisle down which the loathsome slug
came slithering toward him.

Cold sweat slicked the old man's bald brow. It ran down
the insides of his thighs and down his bony ribs. Fear and
loathing such as he had never before experienced or even
imagined rose within his heart. Sick with horror and disgust,
he stared into the soulless glare of those inhuman eyes, and
watched the most hideous death known to him as it crept to
his very feet.

Now that wriggling proboscis touched the toe of his boot,
all the while holding him entranced and helpless with the
glare of its unwinking multiple eyes.

He endured the sensation—although his skin crawled and
sickness was in the pit of his belly—as it fumbled at his feet.

Then—horribly!—it reared up before him with a lithe,
snaky motion ghastly to watch.

For one unbearable instant those hideous eyes stared at the
same level directly into his own.

And then it was upon him, and the Professor felt his con-
sciousness dim into roiling blackness as he sank into the
loathsome embrace.

And he knew no more.

I must now turn back from the course of my narrative to
recount certain events which transpired only a little earlier. If
you have perused the first portion of the story of my adventures in Zanthodon the Underground World, you will recall
how the Professor and the young Stone Age boy, Jorn the
Hunter, found a narrow pass which wound through the cliffy
walls of the Peaks of Peril, and how they emerged to view
the shore and the lagoon and the amazing vessel of the Barbary pirates—whose presence here in the Underground World
neither of them had ever suspected.

When Jorn exited from the mountain pass just in time to
see his lost Princess borne a naked and helpless captive
aboard the pirate galley, the brave cave boy did not for one
moment hesitate to spring to her rescue.

Without a word to his companion, the warrior flung his
lean, strong body into the seething waters that boiled in the
wake of the Moorish galley.

As the half-naked lad clove the waves, heading directly for the strange ship—whose like he and his people had never seen before—the sailors along the rail caught sight of him and raised their voices to hail their captain, who had just come aboard, burdened with the struggling cave girl.

"O, *reis* Kâiradine! Behold!" they shouted, pointing. And the hawklike gaze of the Barbary pirate had narrowed, considering. He could not help admiring with faint astonishment the reckless and foolhardy daring of the savage boy, to strive singlehandedly to rescue the savage girl whom Kâiradine presumed to be his jungle sweetheart. But he wished to be gone from this place, and to enjoy his prize at leisure.

Therefore he had raised his jeweled hand carelessly in a languid gesture. And in the next instant his pirates unlimbered their horn bows, nocking barbed and deadly arrows and drawing the bows until the feathered shaft nestled against their ears.

An instant before the murderous rain of arrows hissed about him, Jorn sucked in a deep, hasty breath, and dove to the shallow bottom of the lagoon. He had just sunk into the depths as the deadly hail tore the muddy waters to froth. So closely simultaneous had been his diving to the bottom and the fall of the vicious barbed rain directly where his body had been but an instant before, that the sailors, squinting into the bright, dancing waters, believed they had slain the youth.

Moments later, the pirate galley came about into the breeze and swung out into the bosom of the Sogar-Jad. But, unbeknownst to any aboard the vessel, clinging to the keel was a stalwart youth with murder in his heart.

Pausing only to catch his breath, Jorn swung himself up out of the fuming wake and clambered up the rudder to a position just below the windows of the captain's cabin, which gave forth a view of the ship's wake.

Clutching the wooden sill in strong, wet hands, Jorn levered himself up and peered through the panes to see Darya struggling naked on the bed with the corsair towering above her, one heavy hand raised to deal the girl a resounding buffet.

Thus had Jorn, without a moment's pause for thought, pulled himself up and hurled through the swinging windows to spring upon the astounded Barbary pirate like a striking leopard. He bore the larger man to the floor beneath the impact of his hurtling weight, and in the next instant his strong hands locked about the throat of the corsair, just beneath his thin fringe of red beard.

As Kâiradine kicked and struggled, striking Jorn about the face and shoulders, the savage boy buried his face in the pirate's breast to avoid his stinging blows; and all the while his sinewy hands closed upon the throat of his gasping adversary with throttling pressure.

As for the pirate, his mouth was open, froth beading his thin lips and flecking his fringe of trim beard. His face blackened as he strove with starved and laboring lungs to suck in one precious breath of air, and a red mist darkened before his gaze while a stealthy numbness crept like some insidious venom through his veins. Taller and stronger was the older man, and in an even match there was little doubt that Kâiradine would, with some effort and a bit of good luck, have been able to best the savage youth.

But when the boy's leap had bowled the pirate over, his turbaned brow had struck the edge of the bunk with stunning force. Half unconscious from the numbing blow, even the sinewy strength of the pirate chieftain was of little avail against the tigerish fury of the cave boy. And this terrible truth burned like a branding iron through the darkening brain of Kâiradine Redbeard as he sank into swirling darkness and knew no more.

"*Reis?* Lord Kâiradine? Is aught amiss?" came startled voices at the door, and the drumming of pounding fists. It was obvious that the noise of their struggle had aroused the pirate's crew to the defense of their chieftain. Reluctantly, Jorn let his crushing grip loosen about the throat of the pirate. Automatically, the unconscious corsair drank into his starved lungs a delicious gulp of fresh sea air.

"Jorn!" cried Darya, springing from the bunk. "We must be gone from here before they come to aid him—"

The boy nodded. Seizing up Darya, he flung her through the open window. As she fell into the sea he sprang upon the sill, and launched his lithe bronzed body after her.

In an instant, both had vanished in the boiling waters of the ship's wake. And when, a moment later, the wild-eyed corsairs burst into the cabin to find their captain half-throttled and semi-conscious on the floor and his young captive vanished as if into thin air, the superstitious pirates rolled their eyes in fright at each other, and mumbled half-forgotten texts from the *Book of the Prophet*.

In their tension and excitement, the corsairs did not notice that the rear windows of the cabin were even at that moment swinging slowly shut as the pirate galley pitched to the roll of the waves. Had Jorn burst through the portal, smashing his way into the cabin in a shower of shattering glass, the sailors would at once have realized the method of exit employed by the captive cave girl. But this had not been necessary, for Jorn had thrust the windows open with a nudge of his shoulders as he had levered himself up to the sill.

Hence the vanishing of the girl was a mystery which struck uncanny fear into their wild and untutored hearts.

For a grown man, in the full noontide of his strength, to be beaten to the floor and half-strangled to death by a mere slip of a wench scarcely out of her teens—who then inexplicably dissolved into empty air, leaving not a trace behind—caused the pirates to recall, with a shuddering foreboding, every weird and frightful legend they had ever heard whispered of the fearsome and mysterious Jinn.

Part Two

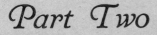

THE PEAKS OF PERIL

Chapter 6.

ANY PORT IN A STORM

Hurok of the Drugars had not gone very far into the depths of the jungle before he paused to linger indecisively in a small glade. As the huge, hulking Neanderthal stood there, his heavy brows knotted in thought, his mighty form dappled by light and shade, he made a striking picture. For, ape-like though indeed were his sloping shoulders, splayed feet and long, dangling, massively muscled arms, there was about the simple Drugar an element of natural majesty. Perhaps it was that within his breast the feeble spark of humanity struggled with the savage brute that was his heritage, and that within his mind a dim but vital change was taking place.

To such as Hurok and his kind life is a mere matter of survival, and such feelings and sentiments as friendship, loyalty, chivalry and self-sacrifice are alien and unprized.

However, in even the short while that he and I had traversed the savage wilderness as comrades, he had learned that the softer emotions are not without value or worth, even in Zanthodon. For I had taught him the meaning of compassion and of friendship . . . and as for the feelings he bore for myself, which even now struggled within his mighty heart against the resentment and bitterness of what he deemed my betrayal, his awareness of these feelings also made him realize that never again could he return to the cruel and savage ways of his beast-like kind.

Once the sentiments of civilization have been experienced, even such as Hurok the Drugar are forever changed. And, as I firmly believe, changed for the better.

As there was really nowhere else for Hurok to go, he soon turned about and retraced his steps to that place near the edge of the jungle where we had not long since parted company.

47

Perhaps the Apeman could have returned to his own country on the island of Ganadol to challenge and conquer whatever rival males had survived the stampede and the battle, but of what avail would it have been to such as Hurok had now become to rule a savage kingdom like Kor, for can a man who has once tasted the friendship and the company of civilized men ever again be satisfied with lording it over a grunting tribe of shaggy brutes?

No. There was no place in all of Zanthodon for Hurok of Kor but at the side of the friend he knew as Black Hair. And when once the sluggish mind of my Neanderthal friend had reached a decision, he acted upon it without pause for further thought.

Reaching the jungle's edge, Hurok examined the breadth of the plain of the trantors without discovering any sign of my presence. Nevertheless, since it had been my avowed intention to traverse the plain and to search for my Princess among the Peaks of Peril, he proceeded in that direction. Trotting with an easy, jogging stride that one with his bull-like strength and stamina could maintain without fatigue for many miles, Hurok crossed the plain in the direction of the distant peaks.

Erelong, Hurok discovered my spoor. He at once flung himself prone in the long grasses and sniffed at the marks made in the earth by my sandaled feet. While the eyes of such as Hurok of the Drugars might be relatively dim and feeble compared to our own, his sense of smell was as acute as that of the beasthood from which his people had scarcely emerged. The hairy nostrils of Hurok of Kor could recognize the body odor of every man or woman he had ever met, even as we can remember the faces of all our acquaintances. Thus, satisfied that he had found my trail, Hurok climbed to his feet again and proceeded in the direction I had taken only a little while before him.

Before very long, Hurok espied the marks of other feet than mine, bent in the same direction. An experienced tracker such as Hurok could read much in the small signs of their spoor, in the bent stem of a piece of grass, a disturbed patch of sandy soil, a recently dislodged pebble. And, using that same incredibly keen sense of smell which had enabled him to identify my tracks, Hurok soon came to know that the three men pursuing me were none other than Fumio, Xask and One-Eye.

Hurok picked up the pace and began to sprint. He could discern no reason why these three should be on my trail, but he was sufficiently familiar with all three to know Fumio for a sneering coward and a braggart, who had good cause to hate me, and Xask for a cunning schemer, while One-Eye he knew from of old for a brutal and cruel villain.

And Hurok feared for my safety at the hands of such men as these.

Before long, the mountains heaved up their gray and rocky heights athwart his path. The Korian didn't waste time in searching for a pass through the mountains, for time was of the essence and I might even then be in peril of my life. So without further ado, Hurok reached up, grabbed a handhold, and heaved himself up to a level where his huge splayed feet could find purchase.

And he began to climb the Peaks of Peril.

Hurok did not know why these mountains were feared and avoided by all of the men who dwelt in this region of the Underground World. His own people, who had for long been accustomed to raid these coasts for slaves and plunder, shunned the Peaks of Peril without understanding exactly why they did so. All that Hurok knew was that these grim mountains enjoyed a distinctly unhealthy reputation, and that it would be wise to avoid them if at all possible.

Perhaps the Apemen had at one time clear and conscious reasons to fear the peaks, and perhaps not. To a preliterate people such as the Neanderthals, whose artistic sense is too rudimentary to have developed an oral narrative tradition, it is difficult to pass down information from one generation to the next. All that survives is a knowledge that such-and-such is *not done*; and this, generally, will suffice.

As he climbed, Hurok searched his vicinity with squinting eyes and quivering nostrils, alert for the slightest sign of danger. From the odor of their droppings, he understood that the dreaded thakdols nested in these peaks, and he suspected that the mighty omodon or cave bear might well make his lair in the black caves that yawned in the cliff wall toward the summit.

And while Hurok was armed after the manner of his people with a throwing club and a stone axe and a flint-bladed knife, and while he did not in the slightest fear to do combat with any man or beast that might step into his way,

Hurok was inwardly restive. He sensed, I think, that Eric Carstairs was in immediate danger. And to pause to do battle might have wasted time.

I can neither rationalize nor explain this sense of urgency that troubled the breast of Hurok the Drugar. That a folk who lack even the dimmest inkling of the concept of time should fret over wasting time, seems to me, as perhaps it seems to you, a contradiction in terms. And were this a work of extravagant fiction, I might pause at this point and consider altering the past few sentences in order to prune out of my narrative this seeming lapse of internal consistency.

But—whether fortunately or unfortunately I cannot quite decide—this is not a work of fiction, but a sober and factual narrative of events in which I participated, so the seeming contradictions of my tale must stand unaltered, for better or for worse.

Suddenly the heart of Hurok contracted in a spasm of alarm as there sounded in his ears an unearthly screeching cry.

In the next second a black, winged shadow fell across him as he clung to the face of the cliff, and that shadow blotted out the misty luminance of the sky.

Looking up, Hurok perceived a horrible winged monster glaring down at him as it circled above his head. From its long, fang-lined beaked snout and ribbed, membranous wings he recognized the flying reptile at once for a thakdol, or pterodactyl, as we would call it. If you have ever seen the skeleton of one of these winged dragons of the dawn in a museum or classroom or book of pictures from the age of dinosaurs, believe me, you can have little notion of just how hideous and dangerous-looking they are in the flesh.

It was even as Hurok had earlier surmised: the thakdols nested in the summit of the Peaks of Peril, and a deadlier enemy of man is difficult to find even here in the Underground World.

Veering in a broad circle on flapping bat-like wings, the huge thakdol cruised about just above the cliff, peering down at the man-morsel clinging to the rock face, clacking its fanged beak together hungrily. It was obvious that the dim and tiny brain of the thakdol was striving to comprehend a mystery: man-things walk on the surface or sometimes climb trees, but nothing within the experience of this particular thakdol had ever led it to understand that they climb mountains.

And also the thakdol's tiny intellect was probably trying to figure out exactly how to get at the man-thing clinging to the cliff. A heavy outcropping directly above Hurok's present position made it impossible or at least quite difficult for the pterodactyl to strike at Hurok from above, and the wind currents here among the Peaks of Peril, especially at this altitude, made it difficult and even hazardous for the flying monster to hover in midair while trying with its wicked hooked claws to rip the man-thing from his perch.

Hurok had the conviction that the thakdol was hungry enough to try at least one of these methods very soon. Which meant he had only moments to live.

Just above Hurok's head there extended that broad lip of rock that was the outcropping which I have just mentioned. The Apeman reached up, caught hold of it, and lifted himself onto the ledge—hoping that it would be strong enough to support his not-inconsiderable weight, and that it would be broad enough to give him a place to stand. He could then unlimber his stone axe and face the thakdol on something approaching even terms.

As things turned out, this did not prove to be necessary.

For the ledge which thrust out like a protruding lip was, as it were, the front stoop of a cave whose black mouth yawned wide and unblocked. There were many such caves in the face of these cliffs, and Hurok had noticed them during his ascent.

He had suspected them of being lairs of the mighty omodon, the shaggy cave bear of the Pleistocene. And he did not wish to enter into that black, close-walled hole in the rock and find himself face-to-face with an angry omodon in the dark.

As if sensing that its luncheon was about to elude its grasp, the thakdol gave a blood-chilling screech, and came hurtling down upon the Neanderthal, hooked claws ready to seize and tear.

Abandoning all caution, Hurok whirled and flung himself into the grim stony jaws of that unexplored cavern whose mouth opened like a black portal to the unknown.

For a time, the thakdol circled about the cliff, hungrily eyeing the cave entrance, hopefully waiting to see if its lost luncheon would soon emerge.

This did not, in fact, transpire.

In time, the disgruntled reptile flew off in search of an easier and more accessible meal elsewhere.

And still Hurok did not emerge from the black throat of the cave. . . .

Chapter 7.

THE DOOR IN THE CLIFF

When the enormous leech reared up to clasp Professor Potter in its loathsome embrace, its forepart emerged from the gloom of the heavy forest into the daylight. Instantly the thing uttered a piercing squeal and fell back into the shadows again, where it flopped and writhed as if in great pain.

Now the forepart, that wriggling proboscis-like extrusion, is where are located the two rows of its six unblinking eyes. Perhaps the monstrous slug was more accustomed to the gloom of its under-earth burrows or to the depths of the wood, and thus could not without intense suffering endure the light of day.

Perhaps . . . and, while the luminous cavern "sky" of Zanthodon is by no means as brilliantly illuminated as are the sunlit skies of the Upper World, the peculiar phosphorescence of the cavern roof is still bright enough to inflict acute suffering on the weak and lidless eyes of such denizens of the darkness as the leech would seem to be.

At any rate, the very instant that the wriggling thing tore its gaze from the Professor, the old man was once again in full command of his faculties. Whatever form of hypnotism or mental control the thing had exerted upon the Professor to paralyze his will and to root him to the spot, the stab of pain inflicted upon the leech by its sudden exposure to the open light sufficed to break the spell which had held him rapt and helpless.

Instantly, the Professor whirled about frantically, trembling with loathing and terror, to seek a hiding place or some means to escape from the dangerous proximity of the vampiric leech.

To his amazement, there was now a door in the stone wall.

Professor Potter gasped, rubbed his eyes and stared again.

53

There was no doubting that where only moments before the sheer wall of the cliff had stretched smooth and unbroken, now a black, door-like aperture yawned in the smooth expanse of what he had assumed to be solid rock!

For an instant, the old scientist paused, staring dubiously into the darkness of the black doorway. But he paused for an instant only. Surely, whatever strange peril or uncanny terror might conceivably lurk within the recesses of that black opening, they could not be half so horrible as the grisly doom from which he had just escaped.

He stepped into the opening in the wall.

And darkness closed about him, absolute and unbroken by the faintest glimmer of radiance from within.

"Glorious Galileo, this is amazing!" murmured the Professor in awestruck tones. For there seemed to be little question that the aperture was the work of humán hands—or, at least, the product of some form of high intelligence. The rectangular opening was cut into the solid stone with such skill that the edges of the portal were smooth and sleek.

Marveling at the curiosity, the Professor ventured a step or two farther into the dense gloom.

As he did so, his foot touched a loose stone in the floor, depressing it slightly. A distinct click sounded in the stony silence of the vault. Then there came a whirring, grating sound, as of massive gears rumbling into action, triggered, it might be, by some mechanism concealed beneath the loose stone in the floor.

And then a thick slab of stone slid down into place, blocking the entrance to the mysterious vault. So flawlessly was the stone cut that it fitted with exact precision, and from the exterior the stone wall doubtless showed no more than a hairline crack—and that only to the eye that knew exactly where to look and also what to look for.

"Incredible!" breathed the Professor. And indeed it was: for, as far as any of us knew, the highest civilization which existed here in the Underground World was that of the cave kingdom of Thandar. And the sophisticated mechanism which had opened and then closed the door to this secret place far exceeded, in its use of weights and counterweights, anything which could reasonably have been expected of a Stone Age culture.

Since he had not any means to create a light, the Professor began to shuffle cautiously forward like a blind man, feeling his way through the black, stifling gloom with extended hands. To his left was a rough wall of stone which continued upward for as far as the Professor could reach. The floor underfoot was likewise rough, but seemed set with flagstones at intervals—perhaps as a guidepath through the darkness.

Step by careful step, the Professor followed this path. When there came an abrupt ending of the wall to his left, he felt about and found an intersecting corridor. Here his fumbling fingertips—reaching about to explore—discovered a peculiar contrivance set high up on the nearer wall, just at the point of intersection between the two corridors.

"My word!" breathed the Professor.

The object seemed, to the touch at least, to be a metal bracket clamped to the wall by screws or rivets.

And the bracket held an unlit torch!

It was a length of wood, pulped into shavings and intermixed with some tarry substance which held the wood pulp together like glue. The Professor took it down, ran his sensitive fingertips the length of it and held it to his nostrils for a sniff or two, in order to ascertain these facts.

The really interesting thing about his discovery was that the torch or candle, or whatever it might best be called, was fresh and new. And that the bracket, which seemed to be of iron, was greased against damp and rust.

Now it had already occurred to Professor Potter that these caverns and the weighted, swinging door in the cliff could have been the product of some long-extinct race from out of the past of Zanthodon. But now he held concrete evidence that the caverns within the Peaks of Peril were inhabited today—but by what race he had no way of knowing. At any rate, they commanded a technology superior to anything else he had yet seen in the Underground World.

And this was *very* interesting.

Fumbling in the pockets of the collection of khaki rags and tatters that was all which remained of his safari breeches, the savant produced bits of flint which he proceeded to strike together, patiently, blowing on them all the while. He hoped, obviously, to light the torch candle, and with its light to explore more easily this maze of caverns. For he had no wish to go out by the way he had come in, lest he find the hideous leech thing still waiting for him beyond the door in the wall.

It took longer than he might have wished, but at last the torch-candle caught fire and the tar-impregnated punk glowed into luminance. The light thereof was soft and muted, peculiarly so, but it burned with a steady, dim radiance. The Professor proceeded to explore . . .

I lay inwardly fuming but outwardly calm with my back against a boulder near the foot of the Peaks. My hands and arms had been bound behind my back, which made my present position a cause of considerable discomfort. Moreover, they had been bound so tightly that already my hands had gone numb.

In front of me, sprawled out lazily before my fire, Xask, One-Eye and Fumio consumed the leftovers of my meal at their leisure. From time to time, one of them would cast a glance in my direction. Fumio eyed me with sneering and venomous hatred; the once-handsome caveman fiercely resented the fact that I had replaced him in Darya's affections—all the more since Jorn had broken his nose with a blow of his fist, thus ruining his classic profile which had made him such a devil with the ladies. One-Eye glared at me gloatingly, licking his lips; I have no doubt that the brutal Neanderthal would have enjoyed kicking me to death, and was probably envisioning that pleasant picture in what passed for his imagination.

But it was the looks which I received from Xask which worried me most, actually. This small, slight man of indeterminate age obviously came from a much higher level of civilization than any we had heretofore discovered during our travels and adventures in Zanthodon. And I did not at all like his interest in my gun.

The reasons for this should be obvious. The Cro-Magnons and the Neanderthals are fairly evenly matched in strength, in endurance, and in fighting skills. Hostilities between the two nations of primitives are balanced fairly and evenly. But, should one or another nation—or some as yet unknown *third* race—discover how to make and use weapons as devastating as my automatic, they could conquer all of Zanthodon and exterminate or enslave all other tribes.

Bringing my automatic into this primitive world made me feel rather like the serpent in Eden . . . and it was not a feeling which I enjoyed.

And somehow or other I had the distinct impression that, ignorant of mechanical devices as he might be, the intelligence of Xask was not lightly to be dismissed. Any Stone Age savage can learn to point a revolver and to pull the trigger—you can even train chimpanzees to perform that sort of trick. And if Xask figured out the mechanism, and if the metalworkers of his as-yet-unknown nation were skillful enough to craft similar devices . . . well, it certainly boded ill, not only for the stalwart Cro-Magnons, but also for the poor, hulking Neanderthals as well.

Maintaining an expressionless viage, I was all the while working on my bonds. My fingers were stiff and numb to such a point that I could more accurately have said "fumbling" with my bonds. And since my wrists and upper arms were bound with cruelly tight rawhide leather thongs, which strength alone could not hope to burst, my chances of working my way free were extremely slight.

Especially since I was rapidly losing circulation in my arms, because of the tightness of the thongs. Soon I would lose all feeling in my upper extremities, and would no longer be able to pry and twist at the knots.

Finishing his meal, One-Eye rubbed his greasy lips dry with a careless swipe of his furry forearm and began picking bits of meat from between his teeth with a ragged fingernail. He looked me over with lingering relish, as if I were to be his dessert. And leaning over, he hoarsely whispered a suggestion to Xask, with a gloating sidewise glance in my direction.

But the smaller man shook his head firmly. "Not yet, my friend, it is not necessary. I feel certain that our guest will prove amenable to reason; if, for some reason, he does not prove so, we can always resort to your crude but generally effective methods at that time. . . ."

And my blood ran cold at the words.

One-Eye growled a coarse oath and climbed clumsily to his feet and went waddling off toward some bushes, obviously intending to relieve himself. Taking advantage of the other's absence, Xask moved over and sat by me.

"I do not know exactly how long I shall be able to restrain my companion from extracting from you the sort of sanguinary vengeance he believes long due him," he remarked in calm, even tones, watching my eyes for some betrayal of the effect of his words.

I, of course, rigorously maintained a serene, impassive composure.

"In return for my efforts to hold One-Eye back," he continued, "I naturally expect you to cooperate."

"Cooperate in which way?" I asked, more to gain time than to gain information, for I already had a pretty good idea of what Xask desired of me.

He indicated the automatic with a graceful gesture.

"I wish to learn the secret of your thunder-weapon," he said. "Now understand me well, Eric Carstairs, I have been driven into exile and outlawry by my own people, for they mistakenly presumed me to be a dangerously ambitious man. It was, actually, the connivance of rivals jealous of my closeness to the Empress which led to my conviction, a simple matter of forged documents, unsupported gossip, hearsay and conjecture. But it sufficed."

I said nothing, but thought to myself that this was, indeed, a dangerously clever man, ambitious or no. And I more than half suspected that his rivals probably were on the right track in accusing him of whatever variety of treason they had accused him of. However, I kept my thoughts to myself; when one has his hands tied behind his back, it behooves him to use a little tact.

His mention of "the Empress" aroused my curiosity. I had not until then suspected that any of the tribes or nations were of an order of civilization sufficiently high to enjoy the sovereignty of anything more elevated than a mere High Chief. I opened my mouth to ask about his mysterious people, who and where they were, but he was already speaking again.

"My only motive for desiring the secret of the thunder-weapon is to provide myself with sufficient power to unseat my enemies and regain the favor of the Empress," he said smoothly. "If you will aid me in this, I promise you not only your life and freedom but a high place beside me, close to the throne of Zar. Only, not so close as my own place, you will understand. . . ."

I smiled, trying to look as sly and greedy as my blunt and rather honest visage could look.

"Let me think about it," I suggested.

"I would prefer to have your answer now," he drawled. "Else I fear that I cannot promise to be able to restrain the brutality of One-Eye much longer."

I made a noncommittal grunt. I certainly had no intention of teaching this Stone Age Machiavelli the formula for gunpowder; that would have been a moral crime on a par with giving Atilla the Hun the recipe for mustard gas. My only hope was to stall for time, pretend to fall in, reluctantly, with his plan, and wait for the opportunity to get my .45 back and head for the hills.

Just then a sudden yell made us look over our shoulders. Holding his hide loincloth about his middle, One-Eye came

"One-Eye came charging out of the edge of the woods."

waddling with all possible speed out of the edge of the
woods. His mouth was wide open, revealing yellowed and
broken tusks, and he was uttering shrill, frightened squalls. A
moment later, we saw for ourselves the cause of his conster-
nation.

For there came shouldering through the brush something
huge and heavy and horned. Its shape was similar to the bull
or bison, but it was more the size and heft of a half-grown el-
ephant. And my heart sank into my boots, except that I
wasn't wearing any by this time.

For the thing was what the folk of Zanthodon call a goroth
and the Professor identifies as an aurochs—the gigantic prehistoric ancestor of the ox.

Big as a hill and angry as fury.

And coming straight at us!

And my hands were tied behind my back. . . .

Chapter 8.

AN UNKNOWN ENEMY

Darya struck the waves of the Sogar-Jad an instant after the lithe form of the cave boy had cleaved them, and she sank to the bottom like a stone. Kicking out and flailing about with her arms, she rose to the surface again, whipped back her wet blond hair from her eyes, and stared about for her rescuer.

He was treading water a few yards away. The youth grinned at her and she smiled back her thanks.

The pirate galley, already underway, had already receded some distance out to sea. The two turned and headed in to shore. Scrambling up on the bank, they wasted no time in making for the shelter of the woods, from which vantage they watched as the vessel of the corsairs vanished in the mists which rose from the waters of the subterranean ocean.

"The hunter, Jorn, has the thanks of Darya of Thandar," said the girl in the curiously stilted and artificial way of talking that the Cro-Magnons of Zanthodon adopt when speaking ceremonially.

The boy nodded seriously.

"The-Men-Who-Ride-Upon-Water would have sold Darya into slavery," he said simply. "The hunter, Jorn, was fortunate that he could rescue his Princess from so undeserved a fate."

Actually, he used the word *gomad*, which means the daughter of an Omad, or High Chief, but the sense of the word is the same.

"Not so fortunate as Darya," the girl observed. "And if she is ever reunited again with her father, he will learn of the bravery and devotion of his warrior."

With that, they turned away and went deeper into the jungle. No further words were spoken, because no further

61

words were needed. Thanks had been expressed and grace-
fully accepted, and that was that. I don't know if the Professor is right in his theory that the single universal language
spoken all over the Underground World is the original proto-
type of the Indo-European tongue from which most of our
language in the Upper World descend, but if he is, then our
Stone Age ancestors had evolved a remarkably graceful
system of formalities long before courtly politeness was in-
vented.

Quite a race, the Cro-Magnon. . . .

Like the simple children of nature that they were, the boy
and girl immediately set about gathering the necessities for
their survival. Jorn had nothing but his sandals and a bit of
tanned hide twisted about his loins. All of his weapons had
been lost by this time. And Darya, of course, had nothing at
all along the lines of weapons or even clothing, for she was
stark naked. Therefore, weapons were the first order of the
day.

Stripping a vine from one of the trees, Darya's nimble fingers peeled a strip length of tough, supple fiber from which in
no time at all she had devised a rude but serviceable sling.
Smooth pebbles selected from the bottom of the brook pro-
vided her with missiles for it. It was not much of a
weapon—it certainly wouldn't do much to stop or even slow
down a charging triceratops—but it was better than nothing
at all.

While the cave girl was putting together her own arma-
ment, Jorn was busied with some prehistoric variety of bamboo. A long, hollow tube-like length would provide him with
a fairly efficient spear—once he had ground one end to a
point by rubbing it against a flat rough stone and hardened
the point by baking it in a fire.

As he worked on his javelin, the girl went hunting, soon returning with a brace of zomak brought down by her sling;
she looked flushed and triumphant.

The zomak is what Darya's people call the archaeopteryx,
the beaked and toothy ancestor of bird life. I have eaten
them and I can assure you that they are edible . . . not exactly a treat for the gourmet palate, understand, but edible.

While Jorn ground the end of his bamboo spear into a
point, Darya built a fire. Flinty pebbles struck together,
shooting sparks into handfuls of dry grass and leaves, is
about the only way the Cro-Magnons know how to make fire.

It is laborious and wearisome, but it can be done. And, since Darya knew of no easier way, she went about her task with serene patience.

Before long the zomaks were broiling on a spit made of twigs which Darya turned over a bed of sizzling coals, while Jorn baked his spear point until it was dry and hard. Then they made a simple but satisfying meal, and rested for a time, recounting to one another the adventures since they had parted. Jorn was surprised that Darya had never before heard of the Barbary pirates.

"Surely, my Princess has heard the old women of Thandar tell of the Men-That-Ride-Upon-Water?" he murmured. The maiden shrugged.

"It is not fitting for the daughter of the Omad to listen to the tales of old women," she said disdainfully. And Jorn could think of no reply to that.

She told him how she had escaped from the a thakdol which had carried her off to its nest in the Peaks of Peril, and of how she had climbed down the face of one of the mountains, entered within the mountain by means of a cavernous opening and found her way to the surface again by labyrinthine spaces within the mountain itself.

"The Peaks of Peril are hollow," Darya observed, "and may contain strange, unwholesome things. We would be well gone from this region, which fully deserves its reputation."

The youth nodded somberly, agreeing with her.

"Besides, the Men-That-Ride-Upon-Water may come after us, seeking her that fled from the embrace of their chief," he added.

The girl shuddered, then bit her lip. But she said nothing. For the truth of the matter was that it had been a very long time since either of them had slept. (Due to the timelessness of Zanthodon, neither the boy nor the girl could estimate how long a time it had been, but the weariness of their bodies was such that they were aware they must sleep before going on.)

"They will not search for us here," yawned Darya sleepily. Then she and Jorn curled up beneath a broad-leaved bush and fell at once into the deep and dreamless sleep that comes to young people of flawless health and untroubled conscience.

Some time later they awoke, made their ablutions in the stream, gathered their new weapons and a supply of zomak meat wrapped in broad, rubbery leaves from the bush under

which they had slumbered. They struck out due "north,"
where a wooded promontory curved out to shelter the lagoon.
It was their intention to go in this particular direction, because neither of them wished to be taken captive again by the
Drugars. Of course, neither Jorn nor Darya had any way of
knowing that most of the Drugars had already been trampled
to death beneath the thundering weight of the wooly mammoths when they stampeded.

They went along through the jungle at an easy, jogging
stride, and sometimes the boy took the lead, his spear held at
the ready, and sometimes it was the girl who assumed the
fore position.

At this point I would call your attention to the perfectly
natural behavior of these two "savages." The boy was handsome, stalwart and lusty. The girl was stunningly beautiful,
very desirable, completely nude. And they were alone in the
jungle, thoroughly lost. . . .

Darya behaved as if her nudity were a natural condition,
which of course it was. But she was neither shocked nor dis-
concerted at having nothing to cover her loveliness: she
seemed indifferent to the fact that she was naked in front of
a young man.

As for Jorn the Hunter, he neither pretended not to notice
her nakedness nor did he steal sly, surreptitious, gloating
glances at the beauty laid bare before his gaze. He treated the
matter with calm indifference.

And he treated the girl with respectful protectiveness. In
part this may have been explained by the differences in their
social standing—but only in part. That is, the maiden was the
daughter of his High Chief and therefore beyond the reach as
such as he, a young, unfledged huntsman, not yet a full warrior of Thandar.

But I am convinced that there was more in it than that.
Perhaps it was the natural chivalry of the Cro-Magnon, the
rudimentary and unspoken but nonetheless very powerful
code of behavior that says—in our modern world and in the
forest primeval—that a gentleman does not take advantage of
a princess in distress.

And Jorn was a gentleman through and through.

While Darya was every inch a princess. . . .

By one of those curious coincidences with which both ev-
eryday life and extravagant fiction are filled, Jorn and Darya

took the very same path across the jungle-clad promontory that Professor Potter had taken a bit earlier.

Reaching the end of the trail, finding the same blank wall of stone rise up in their path as had he, they were at least luckier than the old scientist in not encountering the monstrous leech. But they could go no farther.

Unlike the old man, the pair were young and supple and strong. So they decided, quite simply, to climb the wall of stone. A bit farther on along the wall, the surface became more broken and irregular, which afforded them toeholds and fingerholds.

Slinging his makeshift spear about his shoulders by a length of fibrous vine, Jorn ascended the sheer face of the rock carefully but at moderate speed. Darya followed after, watching to see where her companion placed his toes and fingers.

Before very long, they reached the ridge line of the rocky hills. Like a stony spine, the ridge ran the length of the promontory. Beyond its farther side, they could see naught but the misty waters of the Sogar-Jad, and a line of coast meandering "north" as far as they both could see. Nowhere did they observe the slightest sign of man or the habitations of men.

After a brief consultation, while they stretched out to rest their limbs and regain their breath, they decided to follow the ridge line back to the base of the promontory, where it joined the soaring bulk of the Peaks of Peril. From that point they planned to strike due "north" until they had gotten sufficiently far away from the last place they had known the Drugars to be, whereupon they would circle about the Peaks, and descend "south" again, hoping to meet one or another of their lost friends along the way.

Presently, Jorn became aware that they were being watched. Exactly how he knew this even Jorn could not have said. The men of his race, huntsmen and warriors all, survive in a world of hostile jungles and ferocious monsters only by developing that sixth sense that alerts its possessor to the fact that unseen eyes are scrutinizing him from some place of concealment. Glancing around in all directions, Jorn could perceive nothing that seemed suspicious.

They continued along the ridge line, scanning the skies for any sign of the thakdols that nested in these mountains.

Jorn said nothing of his suspicions to Darya, as there was

little to gain in alarming her. Anyway, he more than half suspected that she, too, had sensed that they were under observation. They were sprung, after all, from the same tribe and it was only reasonable to expect her senses to be only a little less keen than his own. The women of Thandar are no pampered weaklings: in time of war they have been known to stand and fight alongside their men.

If Darya suspected that they were being secretly watched, she said nothing of it to her companion.

Jorn narrowly scrutinized their surroundings. The ridge line they were crossing was of smooth, barren rock, with no cave openings or fissures discernible. There did not seem to be any place for an unseen enemy to conceal himself, nor could the boy discover any vantage point from which their activities could be observed. The jungle which grew thick against the sides of the ridge would be a perfect place for an enemy—whether beast or human—to watch them from, of course. But if any foe concealed himself or itself amid the vegetation, it would have to emerge into plain view and scale the cliffs in order to attack them, and they would have the advantage of being able to see their enemy before he could strike.

It wasn't much of an advantage, of course, but it was the best they had, and certainly better than nothing.

He mightily wished he had a bow and quiver of arrows. But if wishes caused miracles to happen, they would both long since have been safely home among their friends.

Then suddenly Jorn realized with a numbing shock that the enemy whose presence he had sensed had been *under their feet* all the while!

For the ledge of rock onto which Darya had just stepped was tilting on some unseen axis. A black opening appeared in the solid stone as the slab tilted.

Darya screamed!

And Jorn, who was a little way behind her, sprang forward in a tigerish rush, intending to thrust her from the slab before it tilted far enough to hurtle her into the black and unknown depths below—

As the young hunter collided with the staggering girl, she lost her balance.

Instinctively, as a drowning man is said to clutch at any straw in the current, Darya flung her arms about her companion. This threw Jorn off balance, as well.

Then the slab tilted until it was entirely vertical on its axis.

And, tightly clinging together, both Jorn and Darya were precipitated into the depths of the mysterious opening that had appeared as if by magic under their feet.

Chapter 9.

WITHIN THE MOUNTAIN

Kâiradine Redbeard, called Barbarossa, had worked himself into a cold and venomous fury. The bold and wily pirate chieftain was not accustomed to failing to have his own way in almost any matter, for in his corsair kingdom his will was absolute. And seldom did he meet a foe cleverer or stronger or more daring than himself, able to frustrate his desires to any particular extent or for very long.

As well, the Barbary princeling had long been without a woman, and he had conceived of a passionate desire for the delectable person of the Stone Age girl he had discovered bathing in the jungle stream. Sprung from a fiery and lustful race was Kâiradine, and with such men as he, to desire something is never to abandon the pursuit of it.

As soon as he recovered from the surprise of Jorn's attack, the pirate captain knew how his captive and her rescuer had escaped—and vowed they would not long elude his clutches. He ordered the ship about, and commanded the men to put in to shore again. The Stone Age boy obviously knew how to swim, since he had swum out to the corsair galley; and if one could swim, doubtless so could the other. And as neither would have been foolish enough to swim directly out to sea—there being no possibility of succor or safety in that direction—they could only have swum to shore, hoping to conceal themselves in the jungle or, perchance, amid the mountains, long enough to elude whatever pursuit they fancied he might order.

Eyes narrowed, villainous heart seething with frustrated lust and fury, the Barbary chieftain vowed to hunt them down. As for Darya, he intended to beat and ravish her and bear her off back to his citadel of El-Cazar, to make her one of his wives.

68

As for Jorn, he intended to flay the skin off the boy inch by inch, for his temerity in daring to lay violent hands on one descended from the mighty Barbarossa.

As he paced the quarterdeck in a dangerous temper, his first mate sought to remonstrate with him. This was a large, burly, black-bearded Moor named Achmed, who had served his apprenticeship under Kâiradine's own father.

"O *reis!*" said Achmed humbly, "we are under-provisioned and have already been very long from home. Let us return, then, together with all of our plunder intact, and begone from these waters which are the lair of the terrible yith—"

By this term the folk of Zanthodon refer to the great plesiosaurus of the remote Jurassic, which some authorities consider to be the origin of the legend of the sea serpent. And it is indeed a most dangerous and deadly reptilian adversary.

But Kâiradine's passions were aroused; also, his pride was injured that a half-grown boy had struck him down and half throttled him without a scratch. He was in no mood to listen to the arguments or cool reason or simple prudence.

"And the wench?" he demanded between clenched teeth.

Achmed shrugged. "Let her go, my captain! She was a beauty, but there are many beautiful women at home, and we have been long at sea without them. Let us return to El-Cazar, for what, after all, is one woman more or less?"

The Barbary chieftain spat contemptuously.

"She is much to me, white-livered dog of a Moor! If Achmed is enfeebled by age and has lost the pride of honor and manhood, let him take his place among the toothless grandsires and the gossiping women. I am a man—and I will have what I desire! Now dispatch the search parties and get the men ashore, and let us get on with this business without further words of cowardice. *For I will have the girl. . . .*"

Achmed sighed, inwardly stung, but composed his features according to their normal obsequiousness. And turned away to do his master's bidding.

"By the Sacred Well of Zemzem," he muttered under his breath, "it is folly to waste this much bother over just another woman, for one is very like another, and none of them is worth a moment's thought or concern."

But he bade the men into the boats and watched them row in to the shore, leaning moodily on the rail, with a strange foreboding gnawing at the roots of his soul.

For Achmed was the seventh son of a seventh son, and

was given to inklings of the events yet to come in the womb of unborn time. And Achmed had a cold presentiment that his lord's overwhelming passion for the girl savage was rash and perilous, and would lead to disaster.

Within the black mouth of the cave, Hurok of Kor found naught that lived, although at various times in the past this hole in the rock had been the lair of beasts or flying reptiles. His nostrils told him this, for the sharp, acid reek of guano droppings was harsh in the motionless air, and also the guano smeared under his bare feet.

So low-roofed was the cave that the burly Neanderthal warrior had to walk virtually doubled over, and in more than a few places the closeness of the quarters forced him to go on all fours.

With the first turn of the tunnel, the wan luminance of distant daylight was shut off, and blackness closed about him, absolute and impenetrable. The air became stale and vitiated.

Originally, it had been the intention of Hurok merely to penetrate far enough into the farther recesses of the cavern to be safe from any attempt the thakdol might make to get at him. And he had planned to lurk within only until he could safely presume the winged reptile to have flown off in quest of other, more accessible prey. For Hurok was an old hunter, and he knew that the minuscule intellect of the giant reptiles could only entertain one thought at a time and that tenacity of purpose was beyond their limited means.

But once within the black hole, it occurred to the Apeman to explore his hiding place to its end. Not only would this serve to while away the tedium of waiting for the thakdol to give up and hunt elsewhere, but it was always wise, when taking refuge in an unknown place, to discover if it has another exit.

A refuge that has only one way in or out savored more to Hurok of a trap than a refuge.

Before long the cavern walls widened out a bit and soon the jagged roof lifted until Hurok could walk erect without danger of hitting his head on a rock invisible in the dense gloom. Also, the air began to freshen a bit, which suggested to Hurok that some other opening in the rocky roof somewhere connected with the outer world beyond the cave's entrance.

No longer did the droppings of beasts squelch underfoot,

nor did the quickening breeze waft to his nostrils the stenches
that are characteristic of a beast's lair or a thakdol's nest.

Suddenly, a shower of icy water drenched the Apeman
from head to foot. Ducking aside, he discovered something
far above his head that resembled a miniature waterfall. The
little cataract dribbled from some unseen orifice in the rocky
wall far above; whether it was large or small, that aperture,
Hurok had no way of knowing. But he let the water dribble
into his cupped palms and drank thirstily, for the exertion demanded by his ascent of the mountain had wearied him and
his throat and lips were parched.

Having drunk his fill, Hurok was aware of two further necessities, for rest and nutriment. And, since he could do nothing to assuage the hunger that growled in his belly, the huge
fellow stoically ignored it and composed himself for slumber.
The men of Zanthodon, bathed in the perpetual noon of its
unwavering glare, know nothing of day or night and do not
divide time in any manner. They simply eat when they are
hungry, drink when they thirst and sleep any time they feel
weary.

Hence, it was perfectly logical for Hurok to curl up beside
the rocky wall, having found a smooth place in the floor, and
to yield to sleep.

When he awoke, Hurok neither knew nor cared whether
he had slumbered for an hour or a day, as such terms were
meaningless to his kind. He yawned and stretched, spat
phlegm and scratched; rising, he drank deeply once more
from the little waterfall. Then he continued forward, although he debated briefly whether to continue in the direction
he had been heading or to retrace his steps to the cave entrance.

But, turning in his sleep as men are accustomed to doing,
Hurok realized that he had lost all awareness of direction,
and that there was nothing else to do but continue on until he
dropped of starvation or found a way out of this black
cavern.

As he felt his way along, one hand touching the wall, one
foot at a time testing the floor against ravines or chasms
concealed by the darkness, Hurok resigned himself to the almost certain fact of my death. Surely, by now, the foes who
had pursued me had long since caught up with their prey,
thought Hurok. Whatever emotions this assumption roused in
his heart I will not presume to guess; but he came of a savage race who stare daily into the grinning jaws of death, their

most constant and loyal companion. And men fall to human foes or to the great beasts that rule the wilderness or to disease, while those that survive them go on.

And Hurok had the indifference to such things of which the Stoics boast.

But if he was too late to save me from my foes, Hurok solemnly resolved to see me avenged before returning home to rejoin his people on the island of Ganadol. It was the least and last thing he could ever do for Eric Carstairs, and the plain and honest justice of revenge would at least help him to forget the only man who had ever been his friend except his brethren of the Drugars.

And then, quite suddenly, Hurok ran into a wall.

Well, he didn't exactly run into it headlong, for he was and had been for some time feeling his way along with caution and care. But, quite unexpectedly, the Apeman found his path barred from any farther continuance by a smooth wall of dressed and mortared stone.

That is not to say that Hurok knew what dressed and mortared stone was, for none of the tribes of Zanthodon familiar to him were capable of erecting masonry. But he recognized the barrier to be the work of intelligence, through the regularity of the shapes of the individual stones whereof the wall was composed.

"What men could live here, in the black bowels of the world, shut off from the light of day?" he muttered aloud, puzzledly, scratching his matted head with one horny nail.

Then the hackles raised on his nape and along his spine. For it had occurred to the Neanderthal that perhaps this place was *sujat* . . . and better to be avoided. Now *sujat* is a sort of all-purpose word used by the folk of Zanthodon to describe what we of the Upper World would call a religious or supernatural experience. *Sujat,* to them, describes anything strange, uncanny or inexplicable. The fever that strikes strong men down in their tracks, the dreams that haunt them in slumber, the madness of a disordered intelligence—all of these are *sujat.* The word incorporates everything we would describe as totem or taboo, sacred or infernal, and all mysterious and frightening phenomena.

And a man-made wall, here in this black hole in the side of the mountain, was very definitely *sujat* as far as Hurok was concerned.

He prowled the length of the barrier, touching it gingerly from time to time to ascertain that it still existed. At this point, the cavern widened into a considerable breadth, and so it took the Apeman some time to reach the farther end.

And when he did, he found a door.

Unlike the wall, the door was built of wood, and the wood was old and rotten. It creaked uneasily when Hurok set his shoulder against it and heaved. With not too much effort, he broke it open. *Sujat* this place might be or not, his curiosity had got the better of him. And if *sujat* it was, then probably he was already doomed; and if doomed, well, at least he could have the pleasure of satisfying his curiosity before the taboo took its toll.

The rotten wood yielded before the pressure of his shaggy shoulders, and the rusty hinges gave way with a shriek. Ripping the wreckage away, Hurok peered within. An enormous dimly lit chamber met his eyes, its farther wall holding a row of black, rectangular openings which he knew must be doorways leading to other parts of this amazing hollow mountain.

Holding his weapons at the ready, alert for the slightest sign of danger, Hurok entered the huge open room. The roughness of the cavern floor had been smoothed away and the floor itself was now tiled with flagstones. A faint light pervaded the vastness of the chamber and the light came from odd-looking torches clamped here and there along the walls. They burned dimly, shedding just enough light for the Korian to see by. But it puzzled him that the illumination should be so faint; it must, he decided uneasily, have been the deliberate choice of the as yet unknown denizens of the mountain, for even the Drugars knew how to fashion crude torches from dry wood, and they burnt more brightly than these.

He crossed the immense room and peered within the doorways. Each opened into a corridor, and some of these were lit by the queer torches while others were not. From the unilluminated hallways came unpleasant stench, as of slimy rottenness overlaid with a sickish sweet smell Hurok knew but could not at once identify.

Entering at random one of these openings, Hurok prowled its length and found many doors, some barred and some unbarred. Peering cautiously within several of these he discovered them to be storerooms filled with stocks and provisions. Dried meats dangled on hooks set in the ceiling beams, and barrels were filled with various fruits and quantities of round, hard breads.

No longer need he suffer the pangs of hunger, Hurok realized with considerable relief. Taking down one of the slabs of dried meat, he bit off a mouthful and chewed and swallowed. It was of an odd texture and a flavor unfamiliar to him, but it was certainly nourishing enough.

Satisfying his appetite with the fruits, the meat and the bread, Hurok left the chamber and continued his cautious explorations.

Without warning he emerged onto a sort of balcony without railings which hung over a lower level. Peering down over the edge, he saw a dim lit room even larger than the first chamber he had seen. And therein were a considerable number of panjani, both warriors and shes, all of them stark naked.

They sat or lay or crouched about the stone chamber, some alone and some huddled into small groups. And there were children among them, he saw. They were of a different tribe of the panjani, he noticed, for their hair was redder than his own, their skins much whiter than the warriors of Thandar—indeed, they were unhealthily pale. Also, they seemed listless and wan, as if long held captive by some unknown foe.

Abruptly, he heard the sound of marching feet. And there came into the chamber a number of curious-looking individuals, armed with weapons unfamiliar to Hurok. They were short little men, with bandy legs, and complexions peculiarly sallow, clad in odd, complicated garments such as the Apeman of Kor had never before seen. With harsh, squawking cries and blows of whip and cudgel, they herded along between them the naked, listless folk who had been sprawled dreamily about the chamber, but who scrambled fearfully to their feet as the crooked-legged little men came among them.

They were formed into two lines, the naked people of the caverns, by the barking little men in the odd garments. And it was only now that Hurok noted with puzzlement that the little men with the whips and cudgels had hairless heads and beardless faces, a style previously unknown to him.

And then it was, as Hurok watched, helpless to interfere, far above the cavern floor, that there transpired a scene so atrocious and appalling that it was worse than any nightmare.

Sick with growing horror and revulsion, the huge Apeman of Kor looked on, as—

Chapter 10.

THE PEOPLE OF THE CAVERNS

When One-Eye came pelting toward us across the sward, the monster which pursued him emerged into view, shouldering through the underbrush between the trees. From its shaggy, reddish coat, heavy, bison-like head and the breadth of those massive and terrible horns, we recognized it at once.

To the folk of Zanthodon it was the goroth; but Professor Potter had earlier identified it as the mighty aurochs, the prehistoric and long extinct ancestor of the bull.

For a moment, the huge, shaggy creature paused, eyeing the four puny men in its path. Then, lowering its heavy head, which it shook from side to side, and tearing at the earth with one ponderous forehoof, it gathered itself for the charge. And came thundering across the greensward toward us like an express train.

Directly in its path, and waddling toward us with all the speed his bow-legs could command, One-Eye peered fearfully over his shoulder as the earth shook underfoot from the goroth's tonnage. Squalling with terror, the Apeman flung himself out of the path of the great bull—so close did it come that the tip of one horn sheared through the flesh of One-Eye's shoulder. Clutching at the injured part, red blood leaking between his fingers, the Drugar yelled, curled fetally in the trampled grasses.

Xask, white to the lips, rose to his feet, staring with wide wild eyes at the oncoming goroth. Then, snatching up the .45 automatic, he ran to the left, skirting the edge of the boulders that lay strewn about near the flanks of the mountains. The last I saw of him, he was dwindling into the distance, running for his life without looking back.

Fumio stood there, shaking like a leaf, licking his lips and looking indecisively from right to left. Then he bolted in the opposite direction.

Which left me smack in the middle, and right in the path of the goroth, who came thundering down upon me like a runaway locomotive.

I had been sitting propped up against a boulder, with my wrists and forearms bound behind my back. Now this is an uncomfortable position to be sitting in, and a position from which it is peculiarly difficult to get to your feet, especially without the use of your arms. The only thing I could do was to roll over, which I did, and squirm and wriggle until the huge round rock was between the aurochs and myself.

The prehistoric bull came to a stop just before he would have rammed into the boulder. He snorted thunderously at me, then went trotting off in the direction in which Fumio had fled.

Which left me alive, at least, but also alone. And bound and helpless.

After a while, by bracing my shoulders against the rock, I managed to push and wriggle to my feet, minus a square inch or two of skin which had rubbed off against the rough stone. And I caught my breath, grateful to be alive, but wondering what to do next. A man alone in this savage wilderness has small chance of survival without weapons, and Xask had carried off my automatic.

A man whose arms are tied behind his back has no chance at all of staying alive for very long. I would be a late-afternoon brunch for the first reptilian monstrosity to come stalking by. You can't run very well with your arms tied behind your back, and you certainly can't climb a tree to get out of reach. So the first problem I had was to free my hands somehow.

A little stream meandered through the woods on its way down to join the steamy waters of the Sogar-Jad. And something occurred to me that might just find a way out of my predicament. So I went across the grassy space between the boulders and the trees, waded out into the deepest part of the stream and sat down in the cold, rushing water. I leaned back, resting against a small rock in midstream, so that my hands and arms were under the surface. And then I waited with as much patience as a man can be expected to have when he is completely helpless in a world filled with gigantic monsters and primitive savages.

It took about thirty minutes.

You see, it had occurred to me that Fumio had bound my wrists and upper arms with rawhide thongs. He had bound them tightly enough, I assure you. *But rawhide expands when immersed in water*. And the trick I had thought of was that the stream just might loosen my bonds enough for me to wriggle free of them.

Well, it did work. After a half-hour or so, the thongs tied about my wrists grew slack enough for me to free myself of them. The straps which bound my upper arms were a little harder to wriggle out of, but before long I climbed out of the stream and sat on the bank, rubbing my hands and arms vigorously, chafing them to get the numbness out, and suffering all the agonies of returning circulation.

I was still doing this a while later when a shadow fell over me and I looked up to see One-Eye grinning nastily down at me, a heavy club hovering over my head.

I groaned inwardly: "out of the frying pan, into the fire," as they say.

But, anyway, at least I wasn't alone any more.

As he progressed, the cavern within the hollow mountain became a maze of chambers and tunnels and levels. The Professor was amazed at the sophistication of the masonry, the roof braces, the ventilation. Whatever race had devised this labyrinth, this fantastic city built within a mountain, had achieved far higher standards of technology than he would have thought possible for a world so primitive in all other ways.

From time to time he encountered other humans such as himself. To his astonishment, these paid him no attention at all and merely went about their business, viewing his presence with utter indifference.

There was, however, something odd and curious about them. For one thing, while they resembled the Cro-Magnons in many particulars, and their bodies were as well-developed, as symmetrical, and as free of hair as those of the men of Thandar, they differed from the Thandarians in strange little ways.

For example, all of the Thandarians whom Professor Potter had seen were splendid, strapping specimens of Stone Age manhood, their lithe, tanned bodies in the flower of glowing health.

The people of the caverns, however, were wan and listless, they shuffled about their duties as if enfeebled, their eyes were glazed with indifference, their faces lined as though with suffering. And, while obviously well-nourished, their bodies wore an unwholesome pallor, as if they had never in all their lives been exposed to fresh air and daylight.

Whatever could possess a race this intelligent to spend all of their existence locked within these dim caverns, avoiding the outer world? It was a baffling mystery.

It was obvious to the Professor that, while of the same racial stock as the Cro-Magnons of Thandar, the people of the caverns came from another tribe or nation. The gene pool of such tribes and small clans, he gathered, was limited through inbreeding; and, whereas all of the men and women of Thandar were blond and blue-eyed, the people of the caverns had red hair and eyes that were either brown or green. Well, it was to be presumed that more than one tribal grouping or nation of the Cro-Magnon race existed here within Zanthodon, so this was not in itself surprising.

Professor Potter had become so accustomed to being completely ignored by the pale, shuffling, zombie-like denizens of the hollow mountain, that he almost walked into trouble.

He was about to turn a corner into yet another portion of this level, when it occurred to him that since these parts were amply if dimly lit by torches placed at intervals along the stone walls, he may as well douse his own and save it for a later time. So he lingered to crush out the flame in a corner, and as he did so a harsh, barking voice came to his ears from beyond the corner.

Peering cautiously about, the Professor gazed with horror on a scene of unexpected brutality. A very young woman of the cavern people, scarce more than a child, was being flogged by a peculiar-looking individual.

Now the people of the caverns went stark naked, unlike the folk of Thandar who generally wore sandals and something about their loins. But the male who was flogging the writhing naked child was dressed in a tunic of overlapping leather scales, with a clout of crimson cloth between his legs and high-laced buskins on his feet.

He was bandy-legged and somewhat shorter than the cavern people; also, he was either naturally bald or his head was shaven.

And he bore weapons, while the cavern folk, at most, bore tools or cleaning implements. He was armed, in fact, with a blunt-tipped, three-pronged weapon like a trident, and a whip composed of many lengths of braided leather thongs. It was with this last device that he was whipping the little girl.

The scene of cruel and brutal punishment was of itself repellent; but what made it so shudderingly unnatural was that while the child whimpered and writhed, she made not the slightest attempt to escape or to fight back. Indeed, she did not even attempt to shield with her hands the more tender portions of her anatomy. And it was these portions that her attacker sought out with his whip—the budding, sensitive little breasts, the hairless loins and tender upper thighs, and the round little bottom.

The Professor reddened and glared with indignation. But the other cavern folk merely dragged about their business, not even sparing a glance as the child of their kind moaned and wept under the lash of her tormentor. The most attention they gave was to step carefully around the two.

Now, the Professor was an old man and came of the old school of gentility, according to whose code of chivalry men protect women and do not beat them. He strove manfully to throttle down his instinctive reaction, which was to go up to the grinning fellow with the whip and wrest the dripping lash from him and give the swine a taste of his own medicine. Indeed, he was about to do so when, suddenly, this distasteful scene took on another and even more horrible aspect.

For, suddenly tossing aside the whip, the bald man tore off his loin-clout and got down on the floor atop the weeping little girl. The child made no protest against this assault. The Professor could hear her muffled sobs beneath the hog-like gruntings of the creature violating her.

It was an unbelievable spectacle, and the old scientist could not endure it for long. Foolish or not, he could not look on while the atrocity continued uninterrupted. All of the chivalry in his gallant old heart revolted against such savagery.

Throwing caution to the winds, as you might say, the Professor stalked from his hiding place, strode boldly over to the grunting man on the floor and kicked him in the place where it would do the most good.

The hairless man yelped, more in astonishment than in pain, probably, as the Professor's boots were rotten and soggy, and looked back over his shoulder to see who had assaulted him. Whereupon the Professor socked him with a decent right to the jaw.

The man fell off the little girl and got shakily to his knees, clutching his aching jaw. His eyes were wide with amazement.

The Professor assumed the stance of a pugilist, which he had often seen depicted in the cinema. Cocking his fists, he addressed the man on the floor in a stern, breathless voice.

"I would advise you, sir, to stand up and take your punishment like a gentleman! For I have every intention of giving you a sound thrashing—"

The hairless man got to his feet and stepped toward his assailant, mouth open to ask some question or to make some retort. Whereupon, Professor Potter knocked him down with a beautiful uppercut, a skill he had not until then known that he possessed.

This time blood leaked from a split lip and the hairless one spat out the fragments of a broken tooth.

The Professor bent and touched the trembling shoulder of the child on the floor, who was staring at him with wide, shocked eyes.

"There, there, little girl," the Professor murmured solicitously. "I would advise you to run home to your mommy. I shall see to it that this vile cur refrains from molesting children from here on, for I shall give the fellow the thrashing he deserves—"

Suddenly, and quite unnervingly, the naked child screamed —shockingly loud in the frozen stillness that had fallen over the scene. Screamed, and crawled away from the touch of the Professor's hand with terror written on her pale face.

"Why, why, ker-*hem!*" the old scientist spluttered, mystified.

Looking around, he saw all of the cavern people in the immediate vicinity standing stock still, staring at him wildly.

"My good people, I only—" he began bewilderedly.

One tall, lank individual pointed a trembling hand at him, with fear and loathing visible in his green eyes.

"He struck a *Gorpak!*" the cavern man said unbelievingly. "A Gorpak—"

"He must have gone mad," cried another in shocked tones. "To strike a Gorpak is an act of madness!"

"Perhaps he is a pervert," said another, and this one was a woman old enough to be the child's mother. She looked the Professor up and down with horror and disgust. "Indeed, he *looks* like a pervert," she remarked. "See how he covers his body with those dirty rags, and wears hair upon his chin."

"You are probably right, Noorka," commented the man standing at her side. "Only perverts cover their bodies in emulation of the Gorpaks."

Then, turning to address the hairless man, who sat on the floor nursing his sore jaw and bleeding lip, the last man to speak bowed humbly to him and in a servile voice asked the following astounding question:

"Here is the thing who struck you, Master, while you were using my child. He must be either mad or a pervert. May we kill the thing who dared to interrupt your pleasures?"

"Yes," replied the Gorpak mumbling, with a venomous glance at Professor Potter. "You may."

Part Three

THE HOLLOW MOUNTAINS

Chapter 11.

THE THINGS IN THE PIT

When Tharn of Thandar reached the shores of the Sogar-Jad, he stood there brooding, mighty arms folded upon his deep chest, regarding the misty waves of the underground ocean with a thoughtful and somber gaze.

They had searched the jungles between the plain of the trantors and the sea without finding any further trace of his missing daughter, and now they must decide in which direction to go in order to continue their quest.

Grizzled old Komad, the chief scout, suggested they strike "north" along the coast to skirt the edges of the Peaks of Peril.

"There is no particular reason which Komad can offer his Chief for going in this direction," the lean old scout admitted, "but we must go in one direction or another, and I suggest the Peaks."

"There is one good reason," offered a warrior named Ithar, who was the leader of the huntsmen. "And that is that Eric Carstairs went thither when he parted from us." The keen-eyed men of the Thandarian host, it seems, had noticed when I separated from Hurok at the scene of the stampede, and struck out across the plains on my own, thinking to find Darya among the Peaks of Peril. Respecting my right to go forward alone, they had not sought to stay me.

"It is as Komad the Scout has said," rumbled Tharn in his deep voice. "Between one direction and the opposite direction, there is little choice. But before we go down the coast in order to return to Thandar, let us go a bit farther up the coast and see what is to be seen in those parts. Ithar, give the command, for Tharn has spoken."

Without pausing to rest or eat, the host of warriors traveled along the shore where the plain of the trantors ended, and skirted the edge of the Peaks, where they dwindled to mere stony hillocks and small rocky islands scattered out a ways into the Sogar-Jad.

In time they reached the small grassy meadow beyond the peaks, where a little stream meandered through the jungle, across the plain and poured into the sea. They saw a calm lagoon and, beyond it, the long and heavily jungled promontory with its spine-like ridge of stone hills, which was a minor continuation of the Peaks of Peril.

Unbeknownst to them, this small area had been the scene of many dramas. Here it was that Jorn and the Professor had emerged from the mountain pass to see Darya borne off by the pirates; here Jorn and the Professor had parted company; beyond, on the promontory, Jorn and Darya had come ashore, only to fall prey to the trap of the tilting stone atop that very promontory; and there the Professor had vanished into the caverns.

The pity of it was that Tharn was at that moment closer to the lost Princess and to the other adventurers than he had been in some time, and he did not know it.

Hurok, too, was somewhere in the hollow world within the mountains, and Xask, Fumio, One-Eye and myself were not far away at this juncture. Many and widely separated are the threads which make up the texture of my narrative, but at this point the diverging stories of our adventures begin to draw together.

Grimly, Tharn surveyed the empty terrain. Nothing that his eyes could see in the scene before him suggested other than that none of us was within a thousand leagues of this place; nevertheless, he gave the nod to Komad. The old scout led his men to explore the field, the little brook, and the beach. He returned with better news than he had left with.

Tharn followed him to the beach to see for himself.

"See, my Omad, the marks of a young girl's foot in the sand, and those of a young warrior's." said Komad.

"These could be the marks of the feet of any woman," said the jungle monarch heavily.

"Not so, my Omad! They are obviously not the marks of the feet of a small child, nor of an old woman, but of a girl the age of the gomad, your daughter. Neither are they the marks of the feet of a female of the Drugars, for, although I have never seen a female of the Drugars, they may hardly be expected to be any more comely than are the males, with feet correspondingly big."

"There seems to me no reason to assume they are Darya's prints," argued Tharn.

Komad gave him a level gaze.

"These lands do not seem to be inhabited," the scout observed. "And what other young woman of our race do we know to be in these parts of Zanthodon?"

Tharn returned his gaze unblinkingly.

Then he said, "Follow the footprints, if you can."

Under Komad's direction, the scouts fanned out and began to search the sandy beach and the greensward. They did not require much in the way of a trail to follow: a mere freshly dislodged pebble, or crushed sprout of vegetation, or patch of disturbed leafmold sufficed to eyes as keen as theirs.

Before long they entered the jungle, where they found the trail of Jorn and Darya easily enough.

It ended in a blank wall of stone.

From his hidden place on the balcony far above the huge room, Hurok watched as a troop of odd-looking, bald and bandy-legged guardsmen brought the listless, shuffling slaves into even ranks. They did this with cudgel blows and whip lashings, also with angry, barking cries. It puzzled the Apeman of Kor that the panjani did not turn upon the little men and crush them down, for theirs was the superiority of height and weight, and also of numbers. Cowering and whimpering under the blows of their guards, they seemed to lack all power to resist.

Shortly thereafter, when all were assembled into two rows, an old man hobbled forward to harangue them in shrill, hysterical tones. The echoes of his speech whooped and gobbled through the hollowness of the cavern, making his words difficult if not impossible for the Apeman of Kor to make out.

He was of their kind, but different in some wise. Shriveled and gaunt, as pale and naked as were the others of the cavern folk, his stringy arms were clasped about with wooden beads strung on thongs or lengths of gut. These clanked together as he gesticulated. His skull-like head was crowned with a peculiar headdress wherein six red bits of glass or perhaps gems smoldered in the dim illumination. It did not occur to Hurok until later that this headdress might have been fashioned with the fore end of the six-eyed Sluaggh in mind . . . for at the moment, fortunate fellow, Hurok had yet to see his first Sluaggh; the time was fast approaching, however.

After an interminable harangue, the old shaman (or what-

ever he was) shuffled back out of the way and lifted a brass
tube to his shrunken lips.

A shrill, piercingly sweet whistle sounded, making Hurok
wince.

Immediately, a square section of the floor began to lift on
unseen gears, disclosing a scene of such repellence that it was
like a glimpse into the deepest pit of hell. . . .

Beneath the enormous stone chamber lay a noisome, fetid
swamp of black slime and oozing, stagnant water.

Therein squirmed and lazed crawling, enormous, glistening
wet, legless things like overgrown leeches or giant slugs.

They were leathery brown on their outside or upper portions, and their soft bellies were loathsomely pale. Hurok
could see the beady glitter of their little red eyes in the gloom
of the pit, and his huge body shuddered instinctively.

He could not have said why, some primal sense of danger
flickered in his mind, perhaps. For Hurok had never heard of
the horrible Sluaggh, neither had he ever seen one before.

As he watched, nape-hair bristling, thick lips framing an
inaudible growl of menace, one of the leech things crawled
forward to the edge of the pit and fixed its glittering multiple
gaze on one of the red-haired naked men who happened to
be first in line. Without the slightest flicker of expression on
his slack-jawed face, this hapless individual stepped over the
edge and fell into the squirming slime.

In an instant the Sluaggh crawled upon his unresisting
body and clasped it in a cruel embrace. The man shuddered
once or twice as the obscene mouths of the leech's suckers
fastened on his pallid flesh, but made no effort to escape.

An indescribably horrible *sucking* sound commenced from
the slime bed. The whites of Hurok's eyes shone and red
madness flickered in their depths; was the panjani insane to
endure such an abomination? Why did he not fight back?

The sucking sound went on and on. Now another Sluaggh
slithered to the edge of the opening, fastened its gaze upon
the first of the cavern people who stood in the other line, and
overwhelmed her will. For she was a young woman, remarkably attractive, with long curling red hair foaming over her
superb breasts. The dim light of torch candles, which did not
penetrate into the slime pit, gleamed on her smooth flanks
and dimpled buttocks.

Like a sleepwalker, she stepped over the edge and fell into
the repugnant embrace awaiting her. Hurok could watch her
face as she yielded her naked body to the embrace of the

crawling slug. Her features were pale, her mouth open and gasping, but her green eyes were glazed, indifferent, empty.

Again, that hideous sucking sound. . . .

Hurok growled, deep in his chest; his eyes glared redly and foam flecked the corners of his wide, thick-lipped mouth and beaded his shaggy russet beard. He watched, helpless to intervene, as men, women—even small children—stepped forward in obedience to some unheard command, and entered the pit of their doom.

When one of the Sluaggh had finished dining and had crawled from the limp body of its prey, the red marks of the cruel suckers could clearly be seen; they marked the corpse from throat and breast to abdomen and thighs. And the body itself seemed shrunken and depleted.

There were eight of the Sluaggh in the slime pit, and it took eleven of the cavern people to satisfy their hunger. Of course, some of their victims were small children whose little bodies naturally contained less blood than those of the full-grown adults.

At length this grisly and interminable feast was over. Swollen and replete, the gorged leeches lay sommnolent among the corpses, twitching a little as they sprawled lazily in the stinking mud. Again some mysterious signal passed between them and the bandy-legged Gorpaks, and in obedience to their masters, the Gorpaks lowered into place the stone lid.

Then the Gorpaks trooped out of the room. And for a little time the cavern people held to their ranks, but gradually it dawned upon them that their contributions were no longer required. The rank broke up and the cavern folk circulated aimlessly about the room, rejoining family groups or friends, or just sitting down where they were.

There was no conversation between them, and there was no weeping. Neither did any of those who had survived the ghastly feast show the slightest sign of being glad or relieved that they had, for the moment, at least, escaped the doom which was seemingly common to their unfortunate race.

Shivering, sick to his stomach, Hurok retreated from the balcony into the corridor again.

Never in his life had he seen anything more horrible than the spine-chilling scene he had just witnessed. And he knew that it would haunt his dreams for years to come. . . .

And now that the Neanderthal man had discovered the

truth about these mysterious caverns, he was eager to begone
. . . to escape these clammy stone ways, thick with the lingering stench of the fetid slime pits and the hideous things
that squirmed and slithered therein.

Every moment he continued to remain here within the hollow mountain increased the chance that he might be discovered and captured and forced to endure the horror he had
just watched inflicted upon others.

He headed back the way he had come, but the corridors
branched and intersected, confusing Hurok. Before very
much more time had passed, he knew that he was thoroughly
lost.

Stepping with care, slinking in the deepest shadows, huge
stone axe held at the ready, the Korian warrior sought to find
again the huge empty chamber and the broken door of wood
that led to the cave beyond, and thus to the freshness of open
air and clean daylight and the safety of the outer world he
knew.

But the portions of the maze in which he now inadver-
tently found himself were busier than those he had earlier
traversed. The first time one of the cavern people came unexpectedly upon him, Hurok raised his axe and was about to
silence the cry of alarm he fully expected to burst from the
lips of the red-haired man.

But no such alarm sounded. The pale, naked man merely
gazed past the Drugar with dull, uncaring eyes and continued
on about his business. Scratching his head in perplexity,
Hurok stared after the retreating figure. He could not understand such complete indifference to an armed intruder. It
seemed uncanny and weird; almost, the Neanderthal suspected himself to be invisible, but of course he knew that he
was not.

It began to seep into the small brain of the Apeman of
Kor that these people of the caverns were in no wise akin to
the other panjani he knew from the outer world. They were
stalwart warriors—bold, dangerous, fearless, skilled fighters.
But these men, although superficially similar to them in appearance, were like sleepwalkers, seemingly devoid of will or
attentiveness; true slaves, slaves down to the blood and bone
and sinew, incapable of independent thought, without the
slightest, feeblest spark of the instinct for self-preservation or
survival.

He pitied them and despised them. Most of all, I suspect

that Hurok pitied them, although pity—like mercy and fairness and good sportsmanship—are qualities found but seldom among his kind.

He should have known that his progress through the cavern city went not unobserved.

Suddenly, with a deafening clang, a cage of iron bars came crashing down to enclose him. It had been pulled up against the roof by cables and winches, and the trap had obviously been prepared with him in mind.

With a coughing grunt of rage, Hurok threw himself against the barrier. All of the titanic strength of his ape-like arms swelled in his mighty thews as he grasped the iron bars and surged against them. His efforts were, however, futile.

A troop of Gorpaks emerged from the shadows where they had been hiding, to survey the creature they had captured. One of them grinned nastily.

"It is a bull Drugar, in the prime of his strength!" the bandy-legged little man chortled, eyes gleaming. "The Lords will be well pleased, for their carcasses contain very much hot blood!"

"Loose me from this trap, panjani dwarf, and Hurok will find out soon enough how much hot blood your own puny body contains," growled the Neanderthal, shaking the bars until the entire cage rattled and clanked.

A cudgel wielded by another Gorpak rapped his hard knuckles smartly, where he clenched the bars.

"Silence, animal, when Captain Lutho deigns to speak in your presence," snapped this other.

The little officer swelled visibly under such adulation.

"Never mind, Vusk," he drawled gloatingly. "If only the Lords would not take such very great pleasure from his gore, your Captain should be pleased to teach the animal a lesson. . . ."

"Every guardsman in the Ninth knows and respects the prowess and bravery of Captain Lutho," the others in the troop chorused. Lutho grinned, disclosing a row of small yellow teeth which had been filed to sharp points, and for a moment, even through his rage and fury at being caged, Hurok wondered if the Gorpaks had not perhaps adopted tastes in cuisine similar to those of the loathsome slugs they served.

Lutho dismissed Hurok and his growling fury with a contemptuous glance.

"Process the creature, will you Vusk? I have matters to attend to in the breeding pens. See that the impertinent animal serves at the next Feasting. . . ."

All the blood of Hurok of Kor ran ice cold at the hideous import of those casual words.

Chapter 12.

THE UNDERGROUND CITY

For an hour or two, One-Eye led me through the jungle. Although I was no longer bound, I was more or less at his mercy, as the Apeman was armed while I was weaponless. I watched for my chance to turn the tables on the hulking bully, but he was sharp-eyed and crafty, remaining well behind me, out of my reach, and wary for tricks.

I never did understand exactly where One-Eye was trying to get to, for inasmuch as I could see he was going directly away from the island of Ganadol upon which was situated Kor, the cave kingdom of the Neanderthaloid Drugars. I now suspect that he was simply trying to put as great a distance between himself and the host of Tharn of Thandar as he could.

Well, that was certainly understandable.

One-Eye did not spare a moment to search for his lost comrades, Fumio and Xask, nor did he seem at all concerned at their predicament. The two, you will recall, had scattered and fled when the aurochs had charged our camp; presumably, they had run off in different directions, but as to the truth of that, neither of us knew. And One-Eye didn't care either. I did, because Xask had carried off my .45 and I felt rather naked without it, as it represented my sole tactical superiority over the men and monsters of Zanthodon.

However, I had by this point in my adventures lost everything else I had brought with me into Zanthodon, as well as all of my friends, so one automatic more or less didn't mean all that much.

We didn't get very far, as things turned out. One minute we were stumbling along the jungle trail, and the next minute we were surrounded by the most amazing crew of cutthroats imaginable.

They were queer looking, bandy-legged little men astonishingly dressed in long tunics of overlapping semicircles of well-cured leather, like the scales on a serpent; these, plus long clouts of crimson cloth about their loins and high-laced buskins completed their costume. What was so astonishing about these costumes is that, up until now, I had seen no one in all of Zanthodon wearing much more in the way of clothing than brief apron-like coverings of leather or fur—the only exception to this being the silken garments of Xask. Since the sophistication of these garments was so obvious, it would seem that the party which had us surrounded were the representatives of a higher degree of civilization than any I had heretofore encountered in the Underground World.

They were quite a bit shorter than either One-Eye or myself, and were either naturally hairless or had their heads shaven, and their skins were of an unnaturally—even an unhealthy—pallor. They had mean, pasty faces, with thin lips and cruel eyes, and looked in general like creatures who had crawled out from under rocks.

However, they were armed with coiled whips and three-pronged spears like Neptune's trident, and seemed very capable of using them. They ringed us about, yapping noisily to each other in brusque, clipped tones.

At the first glimpse of them, One-Eye turned about as pale as he could possibly turn, considering his natural covering of grime and matted fur, and gulped as if his mouth had suddenly gone dry. The huge Drugar looked scared to death, and in fact he was.

"What on Earth—!" I said.

He gave me a woeful look.

"They are Gorpaks, Eric Carstairs," muttered the Apeman in hoarse, guttural tones.

"And what are Gorpaks?" I inquired.

He looked distinctly unhappy.

"You will see," grunted One-Eye miserably. "Now we are doomed. . . ."

He did not bother to resist as they bound our wrists behind us with thongs and tethered our ankles so that we could walk but not run. Since there were a dozen of the nasty little brutes, and I was, as I have already mentioned, unarmed, I didn't feel like taking the whole crew on myself. So I let my-

self be bound again, getting by this time awfully tired of
being captured every other day by somebody or other.

Once we were safely secured, one of the bandy-legged little
creatures strutted around us, pinching and prodding as if ex-
amining prize cattle.

"A bull Drugar and a healthy panjani," he gloated to an
underling. "A fine pair for the Lords' delectation! They look
as if they had much strong red blood in them," he added,
licking his thin lips with a narrow, pointed tongue.

For some reason—premonition, I suppose—a cold shudder
went over me at this last remark.

As for One-Eye, he moaned, rolled his eyes up until all
you could see were the whites, and his knees buckled as if he
were about to faint. A jab in the buttocks with the end of
one of those trident-like spears brought him to his senses
swiftly enough.

"Yes, indeed!" chattered the underling in oily tones. "Another triumph for Captain Lutho! Two Drugars during one
'wake' is indeed unprecedented."

Lutho preened and strutted, basking in the admiration of
his fawning toadies, and I began to heartily dislike the little
squirt and wished mightily that my hands were free for two
minutes, so that I could discover just how much strong red
blood he had in *him*.

Maybe I should mention that the folk of Zanthodon divide
the endless and eternal day of their existence into "wakes"
and "sleeps." I suppose they have to divide it into something,
to be completely human. Not that these present specimens
looked all that human: One-Eye looked like a gorilla with the
mange, but I preferred his company to that of the smirking
little creeps.

"Vusk, lead the way!" barked Lutho. Then, addressing another of his cringing toadies, he snapped, "Sunth, select six
from the troop and comb the jungle. Where there are two,
there may well be more!"

"Captain Lutho is as generous as he is wise!" remarked the
individual addressed as Sunth. At which Vusk, jealously,
chimed in with: "None stands higher in the esteem of the
Lords than the bold and sagacious Captain Lutho!"

At which Lutho expanded his puny chest as if he would
burst the fastenings of his leather-scaled tunic.

"We have a mutual admiration society here," I remarked
sotto voce to One-Eye, who looked at me without comprehension.

"A what?" he mumbled through dry lips. "They are Gorpaks. And we are doomed."

"Silence, animals!" shrilled Lutho, giving me a sharp rap over the kneecap with a baton-like little length of polished wood he carried in one hand. I said nothing, tightening my lips against the bright burst of pain; but I gave him a Look at which he flinched, licked his lips and retreated.

Why is it, I have often wondered, that while cowards are not always bullies, bullies are always cowards? One of life's little mysteries, I suppose.

With Vusk leading the way, and Lutho strutting importantly along at the rear, where he considered himself safe, we marched through the jungle, which ended in a blank cliff of stone. At some secret signal a rectangle opened within this seemingly unbroken wall, and we were led inside.

I now know that through this same entrance had gone Professor Potter some time before us. I will not bore you with a second description of the black tunnel and so on, but we went the same route he had taken. The mazes and warrens of this underground city were astonishing to me, in that they represented a level of civilization higher than anything I had as yet suspected might be found here in this savage jungle world. One-Eye should have been even more impressed than I was, but he was too terrified to notice much of what went on around me.

Like those of my friends who had preceded me into the underground city within the hollow mountains, I found myself intrigued by the appearance of the cavern people; their unhealthy pallor was only natural, considering that they remained buried here all their lives, never seeing the light of day; but what bothered me was the blank-faced listlessness they exhibited. They went about their menial tasks like so many zombies, oblivious to everything except the job at hand. Not so much as one of them spared a curious glance for us two strangers. They acted as if they were drugged, or perhaps hypnotized, or as if they had long since been terrorized into a constant state of mindless apprehension until they became impervious to every normal stimulus.

In this labyrinth of winding corridors and many levels, I lost all track of direction. At some point we were commanded to halt while Lutho swaggered into a cubicle to report our capture to one I assumed to be a superior officer. This personage waddled out to eye us coldly from head to

"They went about their tasks like so many zombies."

foot; he was older and, if anything, meaner-looking than Lutho, with a fat wobbling paunch and double chin.

"Your success at capturing new animals is indeed remarkable, Lutho," he said waspishly. "Three in one wake is a new record."

"I am gratified at the words of praise deigned to be uttered by one so high in the favor of the Lords as Commander Gronk," Lutho purred—showing that he could toady as obsequiously to his superiors as his underlings toadied to him.

Gronk nodded slightly, acknowledging the flattery. "Put them in with the others," he snapped, waddling back into what I suppose was his office.

We were led down another level by means of a sloping ramp without steps, and halted before a barred aperture. Here our bonds were removed, the door unbarred and we were thrust into fetid darkness. The door slammed to, the bar came down with a heavy grating sound and we stood there smelling the repulsive odors and rubbing our wrists. It was as dark as the inside of an ink bottle, although a trifle of light came from the dimly illuminated corridor beyond our place of captivity.

"Well, One-Eye," I began, intending to make some feeble quip or other. But I broke off at hearing a sharp gasp and a deep-chested grunt which sounded out of the darkness behind me with simultaneity. In the next moment I found myself being squeezed with skinny arms and clapped upon one shoulder by a brawny paw as big as a catcher's mitt. The light from the corridor was dim, but it was enough to make out the features of Professor Percival P. Potter and Hurok the Korian!

"You are alive! My dear boy, how glad I am to see you—what experiences I have had! What a tale I have to tell you!" burbled the Professor, wringing my hand heartily, Adam's apple bobbing up and down with emotion, eyes as moist with tears of happiness as were, at that moment, my own.

"Hurok rejoices that Black Hair is alive and well," said my faithful Drugar friend in deep, solemn tones, with a grin that made his shaggy features suddenly very human.

"Although," he added in an ominous rumble, with a contemptuous glare at One-Eye, who stood at my side, "Hurok is somewhat surprised to find his friend in such low company."

Well, there wasn't much I could say to that.

Chapter 13.

WARRIORS OF SOTHÁR

During the next few sleeps and wakes we did an awful lot of talking. Hurok and I and the Professor exchanged accounts of our various adventures since the sundering of our paths, and even One-Eye grunted a cursory account of the manner by which he had survived the stampede of the mammoths and had met with Xask and Fumio and had followed me across the plain of the thantors because Xask wanted my automatic.

I was, of course, delighted beyond words to learn from the Professor that my beloved Darya still lived, but in the next instant plunged into dejection to learn that she had been carried off by the red-bearded captain of the corsair galley, and that that brave youth, Jorn the Hunter, had been slain. Later, when my misery over Darya's plight receded a little, I would have time to puzzle over the marvel of a colony of the notorious Barbary pirates existing here in the Underground World. But since Zanthodon had already proved a refuge for so many of the mighty dawn-age beasts and tribes of early men, I suppose it was not much to marvel at.

Zanthodon *itself* is the marvel of marvels. . . .

In time we were put to work like the naked, listless, red-haired people of the caverns at various menial tasks, with the beady-eyed little Gorpaks as our overseers. Even while sweeping and mopping and preparing food, or whatever, the Professor and I managed to stay together, exchanging information, conjecture and reminiscences in whispering tones.

Among other matters, he related to me how he had himself been captured by the Gorpaks. As I have already inserted his account of this, how he came upon a Gorpak whipping and abusing a child of the cavern people, while her elders stood idly and uncaringly by, interposed himself, and was

then set upon by the cavern folk at the instigation of the
vengeful Gorpak he had knocked down, I shall not repeat
his story here. Nevertheless, as you can imagine, his account
of his gallantry warmed my heart; if anything, I became
even fonder of the old fellow than before.

"How is it that they did not kill you on the spot?" I asked
when he had finished his story. The Professor shrugged,
sheepishly.

"The mob did knock me about a bit," he admitted. "But
they are so sluggish and languid that I managed to give a
fairly good account of myself. Then another Gorpak came
by, an officer called Gronk, I believe, and bade them desist.
Somewhat battered and bruised, I was brought here not too
much the worse for wear. . . ."

"Which was the Gorpak you knocked down—the one who
told the cavern folk to kill you?" I inquired.

"A creature called Ungg, I believe," the Professor sniffed.
"Venomous little brute! Whenever he or I pass in the corridors, he gives me a certain look. . . ."

"I can well imagine it." I grinned. "They seem to be a
spiteful lot."

"You haven't seen the old shaman or priest yet," he con-
fided. "The worst of them all, on my word! An old skeleton
called Queb; it is he who presides over the grisly orgies of
vampirism they like to call 'Feastings'."

"Hurok has seen the panjani," rumbled the Apeman in
his deep tones, with an expression of distaste.

The scrawny old scientist also hastened to apprise me of
the singularly grisly doom which awaited us in the very near
future—that we would be offered up to the blood-thirst of the
Sluaggh at the very next Feasting—as the vampiric orgies
were fastidiously termed by their servants, the Gorpaks.

"What are Sluagghs?" I asked with rather natural curiosity.
After all, if one is to be slain hideously, it helps a little to find
out who or what the slayers are to be. Not much, but a
little.

He described the enormous leeches in brief terms, and my
spine crawled. At this juncture, Hurok added in his deep
tones a narration of the blood orgy he had witnessed from
the balcony. I felt sick to my stomach.

"And they made no protest?" I inquired incredulously.
"They were not bound or anything, and yet they didn't even
try to defend themselves—to fight back? Great Scot! . . .
granted, these cavern folk seem to be pretty listless people,

their wills cowed and long since broken, but it's only human nature to defend yourself. . . ."

The Professor described the uncanny mental influence which, by his own experience, he knew the monstrous leeches were able to exert over their prey.

"Hypnotized, you mean, Doc? But—can an insect (I guess the Sluaggh are insects) hypnotize a human being?"

We were talking English, the two of us, while the others listened without comprehension; the Zanthodonian tongue did not have a sufficiently sophisticated vocabulary to include such terms as "hypnotize" and "insect."

The old boy mused, tugging on his stiff, wiry spike of white beard.

"More nearly akin to the paralysis-inducing fascination the gaze of a serpent is said to exert over birds," he said, trying to define the unique sensation. "Caught and held in the cold, unwinking gaze of those horrid red eyes, you seem to lose all will and volition, my boy. Ice-cold tendrils slither through your brain, numbing the centers of will and activity . . . the cold numbness spreads to your arms and legs—"

With a little cry, he gave up trying to describe it.

"You will have to experience it for yourself, to appreciate just what it is like," he said lamely. I set my jaw grimly.

"No thanks, I would rather not," I said crisply.

During this brief lull in our conversation, Hurok spoke up, a slow, hesitant question.

"Hurok wonders why the Sluaggh will feast on ourselves next, when the caverns are filled with panjani slaves, who seem to have lived here all their lives."

Potter nodded cripsly, and beamed fondly on the great fellow. He was fascinated by Hurok, and during their brief captivity together here in the cavern city had become quite attached to him. After all, it was rather an unique experience for a modern paleontologist to strike up a friendship with a genuine Neanderthal man. As well, every time Hurok by word or deed demonstrated the consequence of rational thought, by asking an intelligent and logical question, the Professor was delighted. (You will remember his theory that our most remote ancestors possessed the same potential intelligence we enjoy.)

"Ahem! A most pertinent query, my good friend. I have heard the Gorpaks talking and, although their clipped, staccato dialect is a *little* difficult to follow until you become accustomed to it, it seems the answer goes thusly: the cavern folk have, indeed, lived here for generations, captive of the Gorpaks and their own lords, the Sluaggh; they are born and bred to slavery, and, by now, have become completely docile. We, on the other hand—the Gorpaks call us 'surface-folk'—were not born and bred in captivity, and are anything but docile. The Gorpaks regard us with suspicion and, per-haps, a twinge of apprehension. We are quarrelsome, restive, unruly, and have been known to fight back and to strive for freedom from our pens. Thus, whenever one of us surface-folk is taken prisoner by the Gorpaks, we are fed to the Sluaggh as quickly as possible, so as to minimize our poten-tial for danger and hostile activities, such as striving to stage a slave revolt or a mass escape or something."

I could see the sense of it, but the future still looked appalling.

"How long have we got?"

The old scientist shrugged. "I do not know."

After labor and feeding, we were penned for the sleep period in the dungeon. This was an enormous single room in which dwelt others besides the Professor, Hurok, One-Eye and myself.

There were fifteen of them, all told, and they were savages in every wise quite similar to Tharn and his people, being stalwart and tall, the men brawny and majestic of feature, the women splendid and healthy specimens. All had blond hair and the clear blue eyes of Tharn and his countrymen; how-ever, they were not from Thandar but from another tribe or nation of the Cro-Magnon stock. Their land they called Sothar*—but in which direction it might be found, they were not able to describe in words. The people of Zanthodon have, by and large, something akin to a homing sense: generally, they unerringly head in the direction they want to go; but they have no words for the cardinal points of the compass and only a vague sense of actual distance. Anything beyond a march of "ten wakes" to them is infinitely far off.

I first became acquainted with the people of Sothar through one Rukh, a grizzled, gray-bearded chieftain of the scouts of that tribe. We were set to toiling together at various

* The Zanthodonian language employs a single, comprehensive term which includes "tribe," "nation" and "country" or "kingdom," without differentiating between these shades of meaning.

tasks and found some opportunities to converse without being noticed by the Gorpaks. Under such circumstances as these, it seemed, the natural hostility and suspicion between all of the several tribes or nations of the Underground World were more or less relaxed. Strangers in confronting the same peril, it seems, are considered comrades.

Rukh pointed out to me the Omad of his tribe, a magnificent figure of a man called Garth, who stood almost as tall as Tharn of Thandar himself. Among the other Sotharians in captivity were the old wise man or shaman of the tribe, a personage called Coph, who bore a marked resemblance to Professor Potter, being skinny and white-bearded and baldish.

Nian, the wife of Garth, was also among the captives, a superb woman in her prime, who toiled at the most filthy and degrading tasks without a word of protest or revulsion, maintaining a calm serenity of spirit that was truly admirable. Their daughter, Yualla, was a slim, ravishingly gorgeous girl of perhaps fourteen.

These fifteen were all that were believed to have survived of the folk of Sothar; their village or encampment had been destroyed in the eruption of one of the many volcanoes that thrust smoky cones into the steamy, humid air of the Underground World. They had hastily fled the eruption, and had looked on helplessly from a high vantage point as the lava flows from the volcano had burnt and buried what remained of their village. Then, commencing a long trek toward the sea of the Sogar-Jad, hoping to find a new and safer land far from the volcano country, they had at length entered the regions adjacent to the Peaks of Peril, and had been ambushed by the Gorpaks, who apparently launched slave raids into the surface world on occasion, if only to replenish their stock of slaves, which would otherwise have dwindled rapidly before the rapacious hunger of the Sluaggh.

With another of the men of Sothar I struck up an acquaintance, and this was a fine-looking warrior named Varak, who seemed to be about my own age and who possessed a quality of good-natured and playful humor that I admired. To be merry under such dire circumstances would be difficult for the happiest of men.

To another of the warriors of Sothar, however, I took an instant dislike. This was a sallow, thin-lipped fellow named Murg, who was always sidling up obsequiously to the Gorpak overseers with much cringing and bowing, and engaging them in conspiratorial, whispered conversations.

Every nation, race and class have their informers and quislings. I very much suspected that Murg was such. Varak, who thought the best of everyone, did not believe my estimate of Murg's character to be the truth, and Garth himself shrugged it off, saying that each of us must survive as best we can in the slave pens, and that Murg, although not much of a warrior or hunter, was a remarkably clever fellow.

And so I waited, biding my time for some opportunity to occur or for some splendid plan to dawn upon me. For I had not the slightest intention of yielding to hopelessness and accepting these conditions. It is not in me to give up without a fight; neither was it in the Professor or Hurok. Even One-Eye, sadistic bully though he certainly was, proved brave enough in battle. And if the Sotharians were anything like their distant cousins, the men of Thandar, they, too, would fight even a completely hopeless battle, rather than die in the hideous embrace of the crawling leech things.

I would personally prefer to die in battle, facing my foes and doing my utmost, rather than to succumb to the Sluaggh without hope or opposition.

In other words, what we had here was a pretty decent nucleus for a slave revolt. We were sixteen men and three women, and two of the men, of course, were Drugars—superb fighting machines, larger and stronger and heavier than the rest. Although two of the men, the Professor and old Rukh, were relatively elderly and frail, neither was exactly useless in a fight; indeed, the Professor was pretty good in a scrap, once he stopped studying the flora or fauna or whatever, and managed to lose his temper. I have once seen him dress down and thoroughly cow a full-grown grymp, or triceratops, which was about the size of a Mack truck.

That takes guts!

During our sleep periods, unless the wary Gorpak guards were so close that they might be able to overhear our conversation, we managed to discuss the ways and means of escape. Sometimes, when the guards were lax or were otherwise occupied, we could exchange a few muttered remarks during the communal eating period.

Before we had merely begun to explore the problem, however, everything quite suddenly changed. For the better, in some ways, but in others, for the worse. . . .

of the corsair galley: Achmed had seen men flogged to the
bone for less than the disobedience he now wistfully entertained in his heart.

Failure was one thing; disobedience quite another. And
none could be so ruthless or so cruel in meting out swift punishment as Kâiradine Redbeard, called Barbarossa.

So, with foreboding gnawing at his heart, the Moor stood
on the shore, watching with keen and wary eyes as his men
went about their search. He made a flamboyant, even bar-
baric, figure as he stood there, burly arms folded upon his
naked breast, heavy brows lowering in a frown of displeasure.
Achmed of El-Cazar was a huge man and heavily built, with
broad, powerful shoulders and a bull-like chest. He wore an
open vest of red felt with gold froggings, loose, baggy pan-
taloons of pale green silk, their bottoms tucked into the tops
of short, calf-high boots with curling toes, made of scarlet
leather. A wide sash of vermilion and mustard yellow was
wound around and around his waist; therein was thrust a
curved and long-bladed scimitar resembling a cutlass from
the Spanish Main, a brace of hooked daggers, and a pouch of
green leather fashioned from the hides of reptiles.

His head was shaven bald, with a thick, brutal neck, an un-
derslung jaw, broad, full-lipped mouth. His eyes were hard
and wary. Although he thought of himself as a Moor, and
was descended from that people, during the generations his
ancestors had dwelt here in Zanthodon, many racial strains
had entered his blood; instead of the inky-black complexion
you or I would envision upon utterance of the word "Moor,"
Achmed possessed a coffee-colored skin and, among his features, only his wide, thick-lipped mouth suggested a Negroid
ancestry.

Jeweled rings were upon his strong fingers; great hoops of
burnished gold bobbled from the lobes of his ears; armlets of
bronze and gold were clasped about his massive arms; a
necklace of polished but, of course, uncut opals glimmered
upon his deep chest.

Only a few men or women of Moorish descent were to be
found among the Barbary pirates of El-Cazar; for the most
part, not counting slaves and harem captives, the folk of the
corsairs' stronghold were Arab to one or another degree. The
few of Moorish ancestry were to some extent looked down
upon, because of the "taint" of Negroid blood in their
veins—that being the way the other Barbary pirates thought
of the admixture.

Of all his people, Achmed alone had achieved a position of some prominence among the Arab corsairs. This position he prized, as his proximity to the person of Kâiradine Redbeard afforded him vast influence among those who would otherwise have accounted him of little importance and hardly worth the cultivating.

Only one other of his people, a dancing girl called Zoraida, had risen so high in the ranks of the Barbary pirates as had Achmed of El-Cazar. And she was one of the women who belonged to Kâiradine.

Zoraida was his rival for the companionship of the powerful lord of El-Cazar. Were Achmed to fail in this mission, or to skimp in his duties on this assignment, thereby earning the swift and merciless displeasure of his master, it would afford the lithe and voluptuous dancing girl limitless pleasure.

Achmed did not intend to fail, or to disobey.

But always there whispered to him that inner voice which urged him to avoid the search for the girl and the savage youth, for the shadowy and mysterious doom in which that search would surely end.

Erelong, one of his men approached the place where Achmed stood scowling and deep in thought, to report. He was a lean, famished-looking scoundrel called Tarbu, whose long, shaven, lank-jawed face was rendered sinister and villainous by a zigzag scar which ran from the corner of one eye to the corner of his thin-lipped mouth, raising one corner of his mouth into a perpetual and menacing leer. He was dressed in a torn blouse of white silk, open to the navel, whose voluminous sleeves hung loosely about his scrawny torso. His bony legs were trousered in fawn-colored leather, much stained with sea water, spilt wine, and old scabs of dried gravy, which breeches were tucked into high sea boots with silver buckles.

Touching heart and brow in a perfunctory, careless *salaam*, Tarbu reported in a whining voice that footprints doubtless belonging to the missing youth and maiden had been found farther up the beach, and entered the edge of the jungles. Nodding curtly, Achmed took a brass whistle from his waist-pouch and blew a shrill blast upon it, calling the attention of his men. As they turned to regard the Moor, he gestured toward the jungle, directing their search in that area.

"Get thee hence, Tarbu, and show the men the place where the footprints entered the margin of the wild," he commanded gruffly. The scrawny pirate repeated his cursory *salaam*, and went trotting off toward the edge of the line of trees bordering the beach, where a long promontory (which has already figured rather prominently in this narrative) extended to transform what would elsewise have been considered a small bay into something more like a lagoon.

Achmed followed, to take command of the search into the jungle.

But he liked it not; and, with every step that led him into the gloom which lay thick between the tall trees, the foreboding which gnawed upon his heart grew sharper.

As for Tharn of Thandar, the jungle monarch was also upon the trail of the lost girl, his daughter, and on the trail of Jorn the Hunter as well, although the mighty Omad as yet did not know that the youth and Darya were together. Komad, the chief of the scouts of the Thandarian war party, had discovered the same footprints which Jorn and Darya had left when emerging from the waves of the Sogar-Jad and fleeing into the jungles which clad the long peninsula.

And even before the Barbary pirates had beached their longboats upon the mainland, the keen-eyed scouts and hunters of Thandar had followed the trail which the missing two had left as they progressed through the jungle.

To such as Komad the Scout, for example, it was as if either Jorn or Darya had blazed a trail, so obvious were the signs of their passage through the jungle to his razor-sharp senses. A dislodged pebble or fallen branch recently broken underfoot; a smear, where a step had disturbed the heavy mulch of rotting leaves between the tall and soaring boles; long grasses not long since bent aside as a slim body wormed between tree trunks; a freshly broken branch on a thick bush, snapped in passage: these and a hundred other signs, which would have been passed over unseen by such as you or I, gave him clear and certain knowledge that he was on the correct trail.

It is easy to become confused in so dense a jungle as this, whose trees and bushes dated from the Carboniferous for the most part, as beasts in passing through the foliage would naturally make much the same disturbances that the sharp eyes of Komad so easily noted. But here and there, in leaf mulch or a patch of muddy earth, the grizzled old scout unmistakably recognized the footprints of the youth and the girl.

And so it was that he followed, unerringly, the trail of Jorn and Darya through the jungle, to where it seemingly ended at the blank wall of rock I have previously described.

Squatting on his hunkers, eyes narrowed thoughtfully, Komad the Scout paused long as he studied the terrain between where he crouched and the cliff of apparently unbroken stone. The footprints of the gomad Darya and of one other ended here; they did not turn aside to reenter the jungle. This much was plain to Komad.

That there had been others upon this spot, and that recently, was also obvious to him. Those markings he could not identify, for they would have been the footprints of the Professor (whom Komad the Scout had never seen or heard of) and, perchance, of the Gorpaks who had doubtless accompanied into the jungle the monster Sluaggh which the Professor had earlier encountered.

Studying the signs before him on the trampled grass, Komad admitted himself nonplussed. But to his way of thinking, if footprints go to a certain wall and stop, neither returning the way that they had come nor seemingly turning off to either side, they could only have gone in one possible direction.

That was, of course, *up the wall*.

It is, I think, understandably more difficult for even the sharp eyes of a veteran scout such as Komad of Thandar to read the signs of passage up a wall of solid rock made by a barefooted girl and boy.

However, when Tharn the Omad approached the scene, Komad in his terse, economical way announced in very few words to his Chief the conclusion which he had sensibly reached.

It was, after all, the only possible conclusion which Komad could have been expected to reach, since the grizzled old scout had no reason to suspect that the seemingly solid and cliff-like wall of naked rock before him contained a cunningly concealed secret doorway, virtually invisible even to eyes as keen as his.

Turning to one of his chieftains, Tharn delivered an abrupt command.

"Ithar, take six of your warriors and ascend the cliff to its crest," he ordered.

Komad touched the arm of the Omad.

"With the permission of his Chief, Komad will also climb the wall," he said. "On the crest it may be possible for Komad to discern signs of the passage of the gomad Darya."

Tharn nodded curtly in assent, and the climb began forth-
with. Agile as so many acrobats, the scouts of the Thandarian
host, led by the redoubtable Komad, swiftly and with breath-
taking ease began their ascent of the smooth wall of seemingly unbroken stone.

And, from hidden places of concealment behind the
densely ranked trees of the jungle, lost in the thick-leaved
gloom, Achmed and his Barbary pirates watched the strange
actions of the Cro-Magnon war party, their swarthy fingers
curling about the worn hilts of poniard, scimitar and cutlass. . . .

Chapter 15.

STOLEN MOMENTS

From the moment I discovered that Darya of Thandar yet lived, and was imprisoned as was I in the underground city of the Gorpaks and the cavern people, here within the hollow mountains, I would have moved heaven and Earth—and all of Zanthodon itself!—for the chance to speak with her.

Alas, slaves have little control over their movements or actions, and that goes for prisoners of the Gorpaks as much as for any other slave. But, as luck was with me for once, at least, the opportunity I hungered for and dreamed of came within my reach not very long after the moment when I saw Darya and her eyes met mine.

A sallow little Gorpak with nasty eyes, whom I recognized as one Vusk, abruptly nudged me from the line of workers which included my friends Professor Potter, the two Sotharians, Varak and Yualla, and my old enemy, One-Eye. He signaled to another Gorpak.

"Buo, conduct this animal to the place-of-feeding, and give him over to Otha of the Seventh," Vusk snapped.

The Gorpak Vusk had addressed as Buo saluted crisply, and struck me across the bicep with his cudgel.

"Forward, animal!" he squeaked.

I went forward, down the curving corridor, with Buo scampering at my heels.

The halls and chambers of the underground cavern city are very dimly lit, as I have remarked before. Although oil-soaked and tarry torches are used for illumination, they are restrained from burning as brightly as they might otherwise, as the oil and tar are in some fashion diluted with a noncombustible substance. It is generally as dim as the interior of a movie theater here in the cavern city, and I have often wondered why.

112

Having nothing else to do, I inquired of Buo why the lights were not allowed to be more bright.

He said nothing, giving me a sharp rap on the elbow in return for my impertinence in daring to address a Gorpak without invitation. A bit later, he thought better of it, and volunteered the information. The fact was, this Buo was loquacious, like all of his kind, and loved to show off, and strut, and jabber.

"The eyes of the exalted Lords do not enjoy brilliance," he said. "Neither do they relish the light of open day in the surface country nor the brilliance of unhampered fire. This, impertinent animal, is the reason the torches are not permitted to burn without encumbrance."

"Thank you!" I said affably. "I had been wondering what the reason was—"

I broke off as he dealt me a stunning blow beside the head—his way of telling me to be silent. The Gorpaks have manners somewhat less than charming, let me assure you. As I had nothing in particular to gain from further irritating the bandy-legged little monkey, I took the none too subtle hint and shut up.

Buo handed me over to a fat, greasy Gorpak who must have been Otha. Otha was in charge of cooking up the mess upon which we slaves were fed daily. It was an unappetizing sort of watery stew, slimy and half-cooked, and filled with clots of cold grease and morsels of almost-raw flesh, whose origins, whether animal or human, I queasily refrained from investigating.

The room in which I was to labor was capacious and high-ceilinged with fire pits over which huge crockery vats simmered, and roof vents to draw away the oily smoke.

Otha assigned me to stirring one of the pots, while another slave tended the fire beneath the pot with sticks and pieces of wood doubtless salvaged from the jungles of the surface.

This slave was Darya.

At the sight of me, she gasped and all but dropped the armful of twigs and broken branches she was carrying. As for myself, I have to admit I was so surprised I almost fell off the high stool I was standing on, which would have toppled me into the cook pot. Seeing the sharp eyes of Otha fixed in our direction, we hastily dissembled our joy in finding ourselves close to each other again, after our seemingly interminable separation, and dissembled, smoothing our features into bland expressions of weary boredom.

With all the noise and bustle about the place-where-food-is-prepared, and the crackle of innumerable fires, the clatter of pots and pans, and the shrill squawking sound of Otha's harsh voice giving orders, shrilling abuse, screeching threats and reprimands to the others who toiled herein, it was easy enough for us to speak to each other without being noticed or overheard.

"It is a cause of pleasure to Darya to learn that Eric Carstairs, her friend, yet lives," the beautiful girl said tremulously, in low tones, bending over the fire.

"That goes double for me," I said, nor did I have to translate my slang phrase into the more formal idiom of Zanthodonian. For she smiled, her eyes dropping modestly.

"Jorn the Hunter will also be pleased to learn that Eric Carstairs has survived the perils of Zanthodon," she whispered demurely. "Often has he spoken of his admiration for the way in which Eric Carstairs arranged our escape from the Drugar slavers, and the courage and self-sacrifice displayed by Eric Carstairs in turning back alone to give battle to the Drugars, thus affording the rest of his friends the opportunity to escape into the jungle."

"I have good news for you—" I began, then had to break off as Otha screeched at her to return to the bins for yet more wood. Then I had to stand there, chafing at the delay, while she fed the other cook fires and came near enough for me to speak with her again.

"Your father and a host of the warriors of Thandar have not given up the search for you," I told her swiftly. "Indeed, they are probably not very far away even as I speak. Together we crushed the Drugars not very many sleeps ago, with some assistance from a herd of thantors—"

Her eyes lit up with delight and relief at this news, but then she had to continue on her rounds of the cook fires and it was some time before we were able to converse again.

"The thantors were in stampede?" she asked breathlessly.

"They were that," I said feelingly.

"Then it was the old man, your companion, and Jorn the Hunter who caused the stampede!" she exclaimed. "From the heights of the Peaks of Peril Darya observed the two men strike fire into the grasses of the plain, to drive the herd of thantors into another direction—"

"Why do you linger idly by this cook fire, animal, when other fires languish?" demanded Otha suspiciously from behind us. "Hasten about your duty or Otha will lay the flesh of your back raw with his lash!" he added fiercely.

I could, very cheerfully, have throttled the greasy chef on the spot, but controlled myself. Darya cringed, intelligently imitating the way the pale cavern people behaved toward the Gorpaks, and scurried off.

Some little time later we caught another chance to speak. This time I didn't waste words on my adventures since we parted.

"The thoughts of Eric Carstairs have very often dwelt upon the fate of Darya the gomad," I said formally. "And the face of Darya the gomad, and the beauty of her form, have made the dreams of Eric Carstairs warm and rich. . . ."

The Stone Age girl—bless her!—turned crimson in the most adorable maidenly blush I have ever seen this side of old movies. Her long lashes dropped to veil the expression in her eyes, but I noticed that her luscious lips curved in a small, secret smile. She was every inch a woman, was Darya of Thandar. And the woman does not live or breathe, either on—or under—the Earth, who does not enjoy being admired by a man.

"Eric Carstairs has been often in the thoughts of Darya of Thandar," she whispered demurely.

And I felt as if I had just been given the Medal of Honor, the Pulitzer Prize, and the keys to Aladdin's palace!

The next time she came by, I hastened to apprise her of our plans to escape from the cavern city by means of a slave revolt, and asked where she and Jorn, and the other Sotharians, were penned. The jungle girl did her best to describe the location to me, but the meandering and labyrinthine ways of the underground city were so confusing that it was hard to grasp its situation in regard to my own dungeon. Still and all, I guess we conveyed enough information to be able to find each other, with quite a bit of luck.

At that point our precious stolen moments of private conversation were abruptly terminated, for Otha, incensed at Darya's slowness in making her rounds, brusquely ordered her to another task far across the room, and we had no further opportunity to speak to each other.

Except with our eyes. . . .

In the eternal dimness of the cavern city, worked to exhaustion on a dismal variety of menial tasks, it was every bit

as impossible to judge the passage of time as it was on the
surface of Zanthodon, with its unending and changeless daylight.

We worked short shifts of perhaps five hours or so, with a
rest period thereafter, followed by yet another work shift,
then a period devoted to feeding and to sleep.

At some point following my tantalizingly brief exchange
with Darya, I was released from kitchen duties and, together
with some of the listless, naked cavern folk, was returned under the guard of vigilant, mean-tempered Gorpaks to the
dungeon in which customarily I was penned.

That "night" I discussed with Hurok and Professor Potter
and my new friends, Varak and Garth, Yualla, Coph, Rukh
and the other Sotharians, a plan for escaping from the caverns.

My plan was built upon something which had happened
during that very "day," a morsel of information I had
gathered almost idly or accidentally. I had been pondering it,
off and on, during the exhausting boredom of my labors, and
I had perfected it by now. They listened eagerly but judiciously, pointing out any number of possible flaws in the pro-
gram I outlined. And I had honestly to concede that there
were unknown factors which might adversely affect the outcome of our break for freedom.

"On the other hand," I argued, "it is less than manly and
honorable for us to remain here supinely in bondage, toiling
at the filthy and degrading tasks set before us, cringing under
the lash of those vile little devils, when we could break for
freedom, venturing all upon the turn of chance. To go down
in battle—"

"To go down in battle before the Gorpaks," said Garth,
the kingly High Chief of the Sotharians, "is a fate less worse
and more honorable than to yield ourselves into the noisome
embrace of the loathsome Sluagghs. Garth of Sothar agrees
with Eric Carstairs upon this much, at least."

"If we are to do it at all, we had better do it very soon,"
the Professor spoke up nervously. "For there is something I
have not had a chance to tell any of you . . . the next 'Feasting,' as the Gorpaks genteely term the repulsive blood órgies
of their vampiric masters is to take place during the next
wake period.

"And we are all on the menu," he finished grimly.

Part Four

THE FLIGHT FROM THE CAVERNS

Chapter 16.

WHEN ROGUES FLEE

To be lost and alone in the jungles of Zanthodon was no new experience for Fumio the Thandarian. After all, his own distant land of Thandar contained jungles no less thickly grown, or gloomy, or less dangerous than these. Still and all, Fumio felt the cold touch of fear clutch at his heart increasingly the more he pondered his predicament.

When One-Eye had come racing into the little camp with an enraged bull goroth charging at his heels, Fumio had jumped up and fled without a moment's thought for anything other than to save his skin. And, once started on his flight, he had continued running blindly for some time until he became satisfied that the aurochs was no longer in the vicinity.

Such was his panic at the unexpected appearance of the monster animal that Fumio had taken no notice whatsoever of the direction of his flight. Noticing the jungle, he had veered toward it; instants later dense gloom closed about him. He blundered along for quite some time until, panting for breath, his legs beginning to ache with weariness, he paused to catch his second wind and strained his ears for some audible evidence that the goroth was or was not pursuing him. Since the jungle was silent and he heard nothing of the sounds so huge a beast would naturally have made had it been crashing through the underbrush, he soon concluded, to his immense relief, that the beast was no longer on his trail.

Looking about him, the Stone Age warrior was unable to remember in which direction he had come. Every side of the small clearing in which he stood panting looked very much the same as every other side, and in the darkness cast by the tightly interwoven branches which roofed the glade, Fumio could not employ his hunter's gift for reading the signs of passage through the underbrush which a man or an animal make.

Fumio shrugged gloomily, once the knowledge of this was borne to him. Philosophically, he decided that one direction was as good as another. A traitor to his kind, he was doubtless by now considered an outlaw and an exile, forbidden to return to the companionship of his people or to his homeland itself. This being the case, it mattered little to Fumio where he was or in which direction he traveled, for to the homeless, all other lands are strange and unfamiliar.

On impulse, Fumio struck out to his left, where an aisle wound between rows of huge trees of a sort unfamiliar to him. Soon there came to his ears the splashing, gurgling sound a brook or small spring makes; aware of a consuming thirst, the warrior headed in the direction from which that sound came to him. Erelong, he came upon a small brook flowing from heaped and moss-grown rocks. He paused to refresh himself, and wet his face and beard in the clear, bitterly cold water to revive his flagging strength.

After resting for a time on the sward, massaging the tiredness from his aching legs, Fumio rose and went about the business of survival in a practical manner. Coward and bully and traitor though he certainly was, Fumio was also a warrior of Zanthodon; his entire life had been spent in the struggle to survive in a hostile environment filled with treacherous swamps, jungles where monstrous predators roamed and lands in which every tribe or nation other than his own was unthinkingly considered to be the enemy, to be avoided if possible, to be fought bravely if they could not be avoided.

And Fumio would not have survived to his present age, the middle twenties, perhaps, had he not learned fast and well the hard lessons given in that toughest of all schools—the wilderness.

The first thing that Fumio did was to devise weapons. Nowhere in his vicinity could he spy those certain trees from whose long, slender, straight branches—his experience had taught him—crude but effective spears may be best fashioned. However, the foot of the rockpile wherefrom fountained forth the little spring was littered with stones of various sizes, and fallen wood lay scattered about the mossy banks of the narrow brook fed by that spring. Removing a length of leather thong from his waist, where such were wound about his middle to support the brief fur kilt which was his only raiment, he commenced binding the stone which he had selected—the one with the best balance and the sharpest edge—to a short length of wood, thereby manufacturing a crude but serviceable stone axe.

Next, selecting smooth, round pebbles from the bed of the little stream, the Cro-Magnon warrior improvised a sling from another length of thong. Fumio was nowise as proficient in the use of the sling as was, for example, the Princess Darya—the sling being considered a woman's weapon, primarily. Nevertheless, he could employ a sling adequately enough, and two weapons were better than none.

Conscious of that sudden desire to sleep that strikes the folk of Zanthodon unpredictably and swiftly, he chose the crotch of a tall tree to serve as his bed.

With sling and stone axe near at hand, should dangerous beasts come prowling by, Fumio composed himself for slumber, and fell asleep in instants. This is a talent which nature has reserved for the more primitive of her children. It can be observed in beasts and also in savages; men softened and pampered by urban or civilized life seem to have been denied the faculty. But Fumio, of course, was neither, and he slept deeply despite the discomforts of his aerial perch.

And woke to receive the surprise of his life—

While Fumio of Thandar adapted swiftly and naturally to the harsh life of survival in the jungle, it was quite different with Xask the Zarian.

The former vizier of the Apemen of Kor had not always dwelt among primitives such as Fumio's kind or the Neanderthals. Indeed, he had been a citizen of the Scarlet City of Zar which was, insofar as he knew, the premier civilization of Zanthodon. Effete, cruel, luxurious, the men and women of Xask's homeland were as urbane and sophisticated—and every bit as decadent—as had been the ancient folk of Imperial Rome.

While this was not the first time that Xask had been forced to live in the jungle wild, he had learned but little from his previous experience. When, for mysterious reasons he kept to himself, the slender little man of indeterminate age had been exiled and driven forth from the Scarlet City, he had endured the privations and perils of a long trek, as he wandered aimlessly through the jungles and mountains and grassy plains of the Underground World.

That he had managed to survive at all under such hostile conditions, which neither his past experience nor his considerable intelligence had prepared him to face, was largely due to sheer luck, somewhat tempered with extreme caution and wariness. As matters eventuated, Xask had soon been captured by a band of Drugar slavers, who took him back to Kor, where his subtle wit and natural cunning brought him to first the attention and then the favor of Uruk, the brutal monarch of the cave kingdom.

When the same goroth whose sudden charge had precipitated Fumio into flight similarly frightened Xask, the quickwitted Zarian had retained the .45 automatic he had taken from me.

Although the nature and mechanism of the weapon were completely unknown to him, Xask clung to it by sheer instinct. And, when he ran for his life, in another direction from that taken by Fumio, Xask did not succumb wholly to panic, but kept his eyes open. Thus, he knew approximately where he was in relation to where he had been; moreover, glancing back over his shoulder from time to time, the slim little man made a mental note of the place along the border of the jungle where Fumio entered that jungle.

He could not exactly have told you why he did so; taking precautions and constantly adding to his store of information were among the traits of survival which assist one in urban civilization as well as in the primeval wilderness. And Xask—whatever else he might have been—was a *survivor*.

Unlike Fumio, who fled in blind panic, Xask stopped running the instant he perceived himself no longer to be in any danger from the great aurochs, which had gone trotting off, as if satisfied at having driven the puny little man-things into flight. Concealing himself among the scattered boulders which littered the base of the cliffs, Xask examined the situation thoughtfully.

He had not happened to notice the direction in which I had escaped, nor, indeed, was he certain that I had not been gored or trampled to death by the huge bull, because outcroppings from the foothills had blocked his view at a strategic point. Neither did he happen to observe what had befallen his henchman, One-Eye.

Cautiously retracing his steps to the place where we had camped, he searched the turf, finding nothing. If One-Eye and Eric Carstairs had vanished, Xask sagely concluded, at least he knew where Fumio had gone. And promptly the slender Zarian entered the jungles and began his search.

Fumio had not given a moment's thought to the fate of

One-Eye, Xask or Eric Carstairs. Indeed, the Thandarian was rather relieved to be rid of us, for he feared One-Eye, distrusted Xask and hated me.

Things were other, however, with Xask. Unused to daring the perils of the wild alone, Xask desired to find a comrade to stand at his side, and was confident of his abilities to coax or bully or persuade or intimidate virtually any conceivable companion into doing his bidding.

Nor was he wrong in this estimate of his abilities. For the clever little Zarian was another Machiavelli, born and bred. And the secret of his swift rise to power in the Scarlet City, as in the cave kingdom of the Drugars, lay in this natural skill.

It did not prove difficult for Xask to follow the trail of Fumio, despite his almost total lack of anything remotely resembling woodcraft. And the reason for this was the noise which the cowardly Thandarian made as he blundered through the brush in his panicky flight.

Fumio was traveling in as straight a line as was possible, considering the thick growth of the jungle and the numerous natural obstacles. And once Xask ascertained the direction of that flight, he resigned himself to patiently following that same direction.

Soon, however, he became intensely irritated. Twigs and bushes tore and dissarranged the graceful folds of his Zarian garment. Mud and leaf-mulch beslimed his legs and the hem of his garment. Thorns scratched his bare arms and face; gnats and other insects bit him in the more tender portions of his anatomy, and flew into his eyes.

And he began to *sweat*.

Xask did not like to sweat. It seemed to his way of thinking injurious to his dignity to perspire: it was not only uncomfortable but a token of physical labor, and Xask had always avoided physcial labor whenever possible.

He became very uncomfortable. And he made himself a promise that, when once he had caught up to Fumio and had bullied or cowed or intimidated him, he would make him pay for these discomforts and indignities.

Thinking with cold relish on the various ways in which he could extract satisfaction from making Fumio squirm, Xask proceeded through the jungle for an interminable period.

Lacking the great physical strength and endurance of a warrior such as Fumio, the slighter, older man tired more swiftly and was soon reeling with dizzy exhaustion. But he did not dare pause in order to rest or refresh himself, for Fumio was still blundering along in full flight far ahead, and Xask knew that once the man he was following paused in his flight and recovered his wits, he could proceed in any direction—and without creating undue noise which could attract predators. The Thandarians can progress through the jungle as soundlessly as any Algonquin, and once Fumio stopped running and got over his panic, Xask knew he could vanish into the depths easily, which would leave the Zarian all alone.

And this did not at all suit the plans of Xask; therefore, although every muscle in his body by this point ached beyond tolerance, and thirst had dried the lining of his mouth and throat, Xask forced his weary legs to keep moving.

The sounds which Fumio made in his flight had long since ceased. And Xask redoubled his efforts in order to catch up with the fugitive before he had a chance to disappear. Erelong, the Zarian came limping through the wild to where a small spring poured fresh water from a pile of rocks, and the resultant brook went gurgling off through the woods. Xask was powerfully tempted to pause and refresh himself; indeed, he yielded to that temptation, but not without cautiously surveying his surroundings.

And the first thing he saw was Fumio alseep in the crotch of a nearby tree.

The second thing he saw was the enormous bulk of a monstrous reptile shouldering through the brush as it lumbered between the boles of the trees. The small wicked eyes in the tiny head at the end of its long prehensile neck spied the man-morsel slumbering in the tree.

Alas, the tidbit, however tempting, was beyond the dinosaur's reach.

Swiveling its head about, those wicked eyes spied Xask, where he stood frozen by the brook, cold water dribbling from between numb fingers.

The monster had a high, humped back, lined with a double crest of bony blades which dwindled in size as they followed the length of its short tail.

From this, Xask recognized the saurian for a drunth—one of the most fearsome of the predators of Zanthodon and one which, unfortunately, was a meat-eater. I believe that Professor Potter, had he been here, would have known the giant reptile as a stegosaurus.

However, the Professor was happily not on the scene, but

Xask was. And to the philosophical, if minute, brain of the drunth, one man-morsel is about the same as another.

And it came at him like a living avalanche of armored muscle—

Chapter 17.

THE OPENING OF THE DOOR

After Darya returned to her place in the slave pens, she shared the cold, repulsive gruel with the others who dwelt in the same chamber, and composed herself for slumber. But the girl, although weary from the tasks of the day, did not find it easy to drift into sleep. For to meet again with Eric Carstairs, to exchange words with him and to learn that somewhat of the feelings she felt for the tall, black-haired stranger were felt by him in return, was enough to make her heart beat faster and her superb young breasts to rise and fall with the quickening of her breath.

In truth, the jungle girl was not certain how to define those feelings, for the time we had spent together in the slave ranks of the Drugars had been all too brief. And in the considerable interval of time since they had broken free of the Apemen, she had long since resigned herself to the knowledge that I must have been slain. The women of Zanthodon know all too well that survival is a hard and continuous struggle; they become accustomed to the harsh realities of just how fragile human life is in the Underground World as they see fathers, husbands, sons and lovers perish in the hunt or in war, or to hostile nature, with its earthquakes and storms and gigantic predators.

But now—unexpectedly, beyond even hope!—the tall stranger had reappeared in her life; and now her heart thrilled to the discovery that, all this while, he had been struggling to find and rescue her once again. As she realized what that meant in terms of the feeling which he entertained for her, and which remained as yet only tentatively suggested, the blood sang in her veins and the turmoil of her emotions seethed in her heart.

His plans for escape thrilled her, as well; for escape from

this ghastly underworld of fetid gloom and listless slaves was the substance of her hopes and dreams. And, somehow, knowing that Eric Carstairs was near, her hopes sprang to life with redoubled vigor . . . while the black-haired man was not *sujat*, no ghost to walk through walls of solid stone, no miracle worker embued with tremendous powers, just to know that he was near gave her cause to believe that an escape to freedom was at least *possible*.

To be this near to freedom—to hope for an escape into the jungles with the tall man at her side—to know that her mighty sire and all his host of warriors were not far off, and had not given over their attempt to rescue her from peril—all of these were as a potent intoxicant to the emotions of the girl.

How cruelly ill-timed, then, to know that all these hopes were doomed. . . .

For Darya, too, knew that she and Jorn and all of the Sotharians were to be given over to the hellish embrace of the monstrous leech things when next she woke.

Tears came to the eyes of the brave and gallant maid. She thrust the knuckles of one small hand against her mouth to stifle the sob that rose unbidden in her breast.

It would not do to have the others see her weep.

But, O, Eric Carstairs! To be this close to the one she so powerfully desired—and to have her hopes dashed to the cold stone floor!

And, as the little ironies of Fate would have it, at almost that very instant, Tharn of Thandar was even nearer than the Stone Age princess could dare to hope.

His agile huntsmen and scouts had scaled the cliff to its crest. That cliff ran the length of the promontory like a spine, and along the crest Komad and his scouts scrutinized the naked stone for any sign or token that Darya and her companion had passed this way.

Here and there, shallow depressions in the stony crest bore loose dirt blown hither by the updrafts that howled between the Peaks of Peril; loose rock, crumbled by rain and wind, formed deposits of broken shale; plants, their seeds wind-carried to this aerie, sprouted in clefts of the rock; mold and lichen, fungi and moss, nourished by steamy rains, carpeted places sheltered by higher rock.

It was in these places that the keen eyes of Komad the scout ascertained that Darya had passed this way.

It was not the sort of proof that would have been tangible, or even visible, to the eyes of such as you or I. A mere matter of a dry pebble dislodged from its bed by a passing foot, a slithering heap of shale disturbed, the smear of wetness where a hand or knee had crushed the moss of lichen. But to the hawk-like gaze of such as Komad of Thandar, the evidence was blatantly obvious, and he passed the word down to where his chief stood with stolid features, arms folded upon his mighty breast, as if thereby to still the throb of hope within his father's heart.

Once Komad had found proof that Darya had scaled the cliff, Tharn gave swift orders to his warriors to scale the wall of rock. Not all of the men of Thandar were as nimble as the scouts and huntsmen, so crude ladders were swiftly constructed whereby all could ascend to the crest. These were merely the trunks of saplings or of fallen trees, their limbs lopped off with stone axes so that the stumps could serve as rungs.

When six of these were leaned against the stony wall, the warriors climbed in single file. And in less time than it would take me to describe this scene, all were assembled atop the rocky spine of the peninsula.

Here Komad, with every skill and intuition he possessed, strove to follow the meager trail. Since the markings made by Darya and her companion continued for a time along the crest of the wall, he continued along the top of the cliffs until at length he reached the site of the hidden trapdoor which had, you will remember, tilted to precipitate Jorn and Darya into the trap of the Gorpaks.

Komad paused, at the far end of the trapdoor, turning his head from side to side as if baffled. He continued on for twenty paces; then he returned to the place whereon first he had paused. Loose patches of windblown soil lay ahead, and a patch of damp moss flourished in the shadow of a tall boulder. Had Darya and her companion continued farther ahead from this spot, surely they would have left the marks of their passage in one or the other place.

But neither the windblown soil nor the damp moss had recently been disturbed. And there was no sign or token that the lost Princess and her companion had veered to either side of the clifftop to attempt a descent.

Komad scratched his grizzled cheek, baffled. It was as if the viewless air had opened an invisible jaw to swallow the two up. But this was nonsense; ghosts and monsters and witch doctors there might well be, but anything physical enough to have done such a deed would itself have left mark-ings. And no such markings met his eagle eye.

Since they had gone neither ahead nor to either side, nor had they retraced their steps, in what other direction could the two possibly have gone?

That was the question Komad posed to himself as he stood immobile, deep in thought.

He looked down.

The stone slab under his feet seemed as solid as did the rest of the cliff. And he could not discover so much as a hair-line crack that seemed artificial. Nevertheless. . . .

Had Komad of Thandar ever, by some miracle, been able to read Conan Doyle's tales of Mr. Sherlock Holmes, he would have nodded in agreement with that master detective's most celebrated dictum: "Eliminate the impossible. Whatever remains, however improbable, must be the truth."

Borrowing a stone axe from one of the warriors—who crouched on their heels in silent vigil, alertly watching as Komad strove to trace the whereabouts of Darya—the scout rapped against the stony slab and listened with ears no less keen than were his eyes.

Then he moved two paces farther on, and repeated the ac-tion.

Then two paces more.

Suddenly, the sound seemed to him subtly different. In the first two places, the stone had rung with a faint but definite echo to the blow of the axe. But beyond those two sites, the stone rung with a dull thud. Komad looked up.

"The stone is hollow there," he said, pointing.

Without a moment's delay, Tharn gave the proper com-mands to the men who stood eager and ready.

As far as the High Chief of Thandar was concerned, he was perfectly willing to rip the very Peaks of Peril asunder in order to find his missing daughter. And the warriors of Than-dar were themselves no less willing, if only it would enable them to rescue their lost Princess. . . .

From the edge of the cliff, behind where Tharn and his warriors chopped and pried and levered at the rocky slab, the Barbary pirates watched from places of concealment, baffled at the mysterious actions of the savages.

The Thandarians were too numerous and too well-armed for Achmed of El-Cazar to risk an open battle; besides, there seemed to be no need to fight the jungle men. For the moment, he was perfectly content to wait, to watch, to spy upon them, for it seemed that they, too, were searching for something.

It never occurred to Achmed to guess that both his men and the savages were searching for the same young woman.

"What is it that they do, the wild men?" inquired Tarbu in a hoarse whisper, from where he crouched at the elbow of the first mate of the *Red Witch*.

Achmed shrugged, mystified.

"Allah alone knows," he muttered. For it seemed to him as if the savages were trying to break into the very fabric of the cliffs. Although why they should, or what it was they were after, was beyond the imaginings of the Moor.

"Let us fall upon them, and slay," grumbled a burly Turk named Kemal, who crouched nearby in the shade of the boulder. "To lurk like dogs—to slink and scurry—is not seemly for the heroes of El-Cazar."

Achmed gave him a glare of fierce reproof.

"You will lurk and scurry like dogs, O dog of Istamboul, if I bid you do so," he snarled. "They are armed and they are many—"

"No more than are we," grunted the Turk, hefting the hilt of his dented scimitar significantly, his magnificent mustachios (which were his pride and joy) bristling belligerently.

"Still thy tongue, O Kemal, or I shall slit it for thee, and thou shalt croak all thy days like a raven," said Achmed coldly. "It behooves us now to wait and watch and listen—"

Grumbling and calling upon his prophet, the fat Turk subsided. The Barbary pirates had watched from the shelter of the trees as the primitives had felled and trimmed the tall saplings whereby they had scaled the sheer wall of the cliffs. Once the savages were gone farther down the rocky spine of the promontory, Achmed had cautiously bade his corsairs ascend the cliff by means of the same crude ladders. Now they held the rear of the Thandarian host, crouched behind tall spires of rock and round boulders, watching carefully.

"The Barbarossa would not hide like a starveling cur," grouched Kemal to the man nearest him, but in low tones so that Achmed would not overhear.

"The Barbarossa is not here, dog of a Turk," spat the lean Arab at his side. "And the mate Achmed is. So we must do his bidding . . . of what use to engage a band of howling savages? We are not here for war, but to seize a runaway girl. Now be silent, and let us observe in silence. . . ."

Powerful and determined were the warriors of Thandar, and indefatigable. But, for all the vigor of their unrelenting effort, the secret of the mechanism which controlled the stone trapdoor continued to elude them.

Nevertheless, they toiled on.

Tharn frowned, his head heavy. For all the jungle monarch knew, every moment might count. Even at this moment, a horrible doom might be creeping upon his helpless daughter in those black and unknown depths below his feet.

Somehow he guessed that time was running out. . . .

But there was nothing to do but strive on.

Chapter 18.

BURNING BRIGHT

Harsh gongs awoke us from our restless, troubled slumbers. The bars were withdrawn which blocked the door to our pen, and bandy-legged little Gorpaks came waddling between the rows of sleeping men and women, rousing us with flicks of the whip and sharp, barking commands.

When we were assembled into ranks, my personal adversary, little Captain Lutho, came strutting and preening before us, eyeing us up and down with shrewd, gloating gaze.

"Attention, animals!" he snapped. "It is now your inestimable honor to serve Those who are in every way greater than yourselves, as They are in every way superior even to us Gorpaks, their servants and minions! Reluctance and recalcitrance will not be tolerated, for your entire purpose in this world is to obey the least whim of Those who are as far above you in the scheme of nature as you are above the worms that delve in the dark places of the earth. . . ."

The pompous little dwarf went on in this general line for a lengthy harangue, before we at last were herded out of our dungeon and down a winding corridor to our unknown doom.

As we marched stolidly along, I caught the opportunity to exchange meaningful glances with Hurok, Varak and Garth, the Omad of the men of Sothar. During the sleep period just past, we had talked long, laying our plans. Garth had been of the opinion that we should spring upon the Gorpaks the moment they dispersed down the aisles between our rows of sleeping places, but I counseled delay.

"Let us wait until they march us forward to meet their Masters," I had argued. "Both the Sluaggh and the Gorpaks are more accustomed to dealing with the cowed and broken cavern people than they are with brave and determined fighting men. And I have a little surprise in store for the Sluaggh. . . ."

In the end, Garth yielded to the superior wisdom of my scheme. At least, I hoped that my wisdom was superior, but only time would tell . . . and time, for us, was swiftly running out. . . .

At some juncture in the maze of wandering corridors we encountered another pack of captives, who were under heavy guard by the Gorpaks. I guessed at once that this crowd contained the other Sotharian party, and Jorn and my beloved Princess as well. Nor was I wrong: across the heads of the blond warriors, my eyes flew to Darya's lovely face, and her blue eyes clung to mine. I strove to convey confidence in my expression, but I do not know if she saw anything there but that which she expected to see.

We were formed together, and the men of Sothar who had been long parted from their friends and family members in the other group, clung together, happily weeping, until separated by blows of whip and cudgel. But the cruel Gorpaks, for all their brutality, could not prevent the men and women of Sothar from looking into the faces of their mates, their relatives and their friends.

By my side, Professor Potter limped along, grumbling. Behind me, Hurok loomed protectively, saying nothing. Farther down the line, One-Eye stumped along, his huge head lowered, and beneath his russet fur and coating of dirt I knew his ugly features were pale and sweating with craven fear.

My heart was in my throat. This long trek through the caverns might well be the last journey for me and my friends. But I consoled myself with the knowledge that, at least, we would go out fighting. It wasn't as much consolation as I could have used at that moment, but it was all I had. And I wondered to myself if my plan would work. . . .

We came at length into the enormous stone room of which Hurok had told me in his account of his own adventures. All was as he had described it to me, the great slab of a trapdoor beneath which, I assumed, the hideous Sluaggh lolled, awaiting their repulsive repast. Above, I glimpsed the unrailed balcony from which the Apeman had observed the leeches at their Feasting. Around the walls of the vast, echoing chamber, torches widely spaced were set; and, like those that illuminated the rest of the cavern city, they burned exceedingly dim.

Here the Gorpaks left us for a time, although a squad remained on guard at the doorway. We huddled together by prearranged plan, as if for comfort in the proximity of our comrades. And, with Sotharian warriors placed so as to block our actions from the watchful Gorpaks, we proceeded to perform an action that might well have seemed inexplicable to you, had you been present to observe it.

We all took off our clothes.

I have already alluded to the fact that the human inhabitants of Zanthodon are no Puritans. They feel no particular shame at exposing their bodies to the indifferent gaze of others. Indeed, in the steamy, tropic warmth of Zanthodon's eternal noon, to wear very much in the way of clothing is unnecessary and quite uncomfortable.

So it was that, men and women together, we stripped off our few, scant garments. Sharp teeth and strong hands tore the furs and pelts into strips. Agile fingers knotted these together swiftly into a long rope (pray the Lord it would prove long enough!), which we hastily coiled and concealed with our bodies as the Gorpaks returned in force.

It did not seem to me very likely that the Gorpaks would pay any attention to our nakedness. They were accustomed to seeing the pale, listless cavern folk go about their duties unclothed, and, as they regard us as "animals," they could be assumed to be indifferent as to whether we covered ourselves or not.

This remained to be seen; and much hinged upon our hope that they would not notice our state of undress and become suspicious.

Thank God they did not.

Scarcely giving us a glance, they formed us into two lines, and then there stepped forth the bald and wizened old shaman of the Gorpaks, the one called Queb, of whom Hurok had told me. He was a ridiculous figure in his beads and bangles, head wobbling under his fantastic headdress, but sinister enough in light of his purpose.

Queb began to harangue us in a shrill, unpleasant voice, lecturing us on our good fortune to be selected for this Feasting, to yield up the rich nourishment of our blood to the need of Those who were as immensely our superiors as we were superior to worms and grubs. The hysterical speech went on and on and more than a few of us became fidgety.

Finally, the sermon was over, and Queb lifted to his lips

the whistle he wore about his scrawny old neck, and shrilled forth a piercing cry.

The slab rolled back with a heavy grating noise.

And there they were, just as Hurok had described . . . the huge, wriggling leeches sprawled lazily amid filthy puddles of stagnant water and slick beds of stinking slime. My gorge rose at the fetid reek of the Sluagghs' lair, but I clamped my lips tightly together. It would not do to get sick now, with so much to be done.

The first of the monstrous leeches came slithering forward to the edge of the slime pit. I caught a glimpse of its six lidless unwinking red eyes, and felt my mind brushed by chill tendrils of uncanny force. With an effort, I wrenched my gaze away from that stare, but the person behind me was not quite so quick as I to avert her eyes.

It was Darya!

Her face went blank, her jaw slack. Like a mindless automaton of warm flesh, the naked girl began walking toward the edge of the pit, and my heart froze within me.

I sprang forward, seized her by the upper arms as she teetered on the very brink, jerked her roughly away and shook her until her head wobbled.

Still her eyes were glazed, indifferent.

Forgive me, but I slapped her face! Her head snapped back and the old familiar Darya again inhabited her glorious eyes. For a moment, rubbing her reddened cheek, she looked angry; then her gaze softened, as she became cognizant of what had occurred.

"Thank you, Eric," she whispered.

But now others of the Sotharians were caught in the icy glare of the Sluaggh.

"Don't look them in the eyes!" yelled Professor Potter in a loud voice that made everybody jump.

The echoes of his sudden shout bounced from wall to wall. The Gorpaks were frozen with mingled astonishment and outrage, for this was to them, I guess, a solemn, perhaps even a sacred, moment.

I whirled into action.

Balling one fist, I knocked down the guard that stood nearest to me. He toppled over on his back, squalling.

I jumped over him and sprinted for the wall. Reaching it, I sprang up and seized the bracket which held the feebly burning torch. I drew the flaming length of chemical-soaked wood forth, and dropped to the floor again, heading back to the edge of the pit.

The Gorpaks, yelping with fury, were waddling toward me to block me from my goal.

Then Hurok strode forth among them, huge fists striking from left to right like heavy pistons. With each smacking blow, a Gorpak went down with a broken neck, a shattered jaw, a dislocated shoulder or whatever. And behind Hurok came Garth and Varak and the other warriors, hurling themselves upon the Gorpaks from behind, pulling them down and trampling them into unconsciousness.

I circled around the embattled Gorpaks, heading for the edge of the pit. Near it, I crouched, and from the scrap of cloth I held balled in one hand I poured a whiff of dry, black powder over the burning end of the torch I held.

With a loud spitting and sizzling of sparks, a furious brilliance flared up to destroy the twilight gloom of the Chamber of Feasting.

Brightly now burned the torch—not as bright as the luminance of open day, but bright enough! The Gorpaks squeaked and yelped, covering their beady little eyes from the unusual radiance.

At the very edge of the pit, averting my eyes, I held forth the torch. Its searing light fell upon the fetid swamp-like bed whereon the loathsome Sluagghs wriggled. Their lidless eyes, which could not endure anything more than the twilight of the caverns, drank in the sizzling fury of the flame.

And they went mad! Coiling and uncoiling, flopping and writhing, they slithered about in the stinking slime, uttering a thin, ululating cry so high pitched as almost to be inaudible.

I stood there grinning, brandishing my torch, letting its light drive them into panicky flight. "Serves the slimy bastards right," I thought to myself with grim satisfaction.

Now Potter and Hurok came up to where I stood, having retrieved two more torches from brackets along the nearer wall. I handed the Professor my other packet. He sprinkled his torch with the dry gunpowder which last night I had emptied out of the few cartridges remaining in my gun belt. And his torch flamed up, spitting sparks, adding its light to my own. Soon all three torches were ablaze, and in the triple radiance, the Gorpaks stumbled blindly, mewling piteously and trying to shield their eyes. Garth's warriors made short work of them.

"I told you it would work, didn't I, my boy!" the Professor

commented, very pleased with himself. "I thought the powder in your cartridges would unite with the chemical-impregnated torch wood to flare up like fireworks!"

"You can take credit for a lot more than that, Doc," I grinned. "From the very moment you told me about that scene in the glade, where the Sluaggh flinched back from the direct light of day, I've been trying to figure out how to use that fact against them. The only weapon we had to use was to pit their own weakness against them—*they cannot endure light.*"

"Very kind of you to give me the credit, my boy," said the Professor. "I suspect their inability to stand direct daylight stems from the fact that, in their natural habitat, they dwell in fetid burrows deep underground. Doubtless they evolved in those depths, living in utter darkness."

"They're not some form of prehistoric life from the surface world, then?"

"I believe not," mused the old scientist. "We have no fossil record of any leech so large as they . . . no, I believe the Sluagghs are indigenous to Zanthodon and have never penetrated to the world above our heads."

"And let's hope they never do," I muttered.

"Amen to that," said the Professor fervently.

But we had no time for discussion; things were heating up, and time was getting short.

"More Gorpaks approach, Eric Carstairs!" boomed the deep voice of Garth as he came up to us. "Already the men of Sothar have unlimbered the rope—"

I looked across the chamber. While I had been driving the Sluagghs back into their noisome burrows under the floor, the Sotharians had been trying to secure the long rope we had made from knotted strips of our clothing about the edge of the balcony. A loop had been fashioned, and a slipknot. How many tries they made before it snagged the sharp protruding corner of the balcony I never bothered to ask, but it was secure now.

Already the men and women of Sothar were climbing the rope to gather on the balcony. We ran over to where they stood, and I boosted Darya up when her turn came while Hurok and Garth and the mightier of the Sotharian fighting men stood guard at the doorway, armed now with weapons seized from the Gorpaks they had felled.

As it chanced, we all managed to climb to the balcony level before the reinforcements arrived. Drawing our improvised rope ladder up with us, to discourage its use by our pursuers, we made tracks through the storerooms and other chambers Hurok had described.

Almighty God, but it was like cold water to a man perishing of thirst, to be running free through the upper level of the cavern city, with a long trident in my hand and my beloved at my side! Freedom has a heady taste—better than all the champagne in the world!

With Hurok at the fore, we retraced the route he had first taken into the maze of caverns. Erelong we reached that huge, unused chamber that had been his first glimpse of the city of the Sluagghs.

There was the wall of dressed and mortared stone, just as he had described it. The stone wall which separated this portion of the outermost parts of the city from the natural caverns.

And there was the old, forgotten door of rotten wood through which he had forced his way.

A shattered ruin, it hung in fragments from rusted hinges. I smiled with relief at the sight of it; never had any door in all the world looked so damned good to me before. . . .

In less time than it would take to tell, we were through the door, to the last man and woman, and stood in the black and lightless caverns of the hollow mountains.

But they were lightless no more! For still our torches burned brightly, and by their treble radiance we could see the mouth of a black opening in the jagged wall.

"Hurok believes that is the way he came hither," grunted my huge friend, pointing.

We headed for it, wasting no time, for surely the Gorpaks would be yelping at our heels before too many minutes had gone by.

And so began our flight from the caverns, and the nightmare of our slavery in this living hell was over and done with forever.

Chapter 14.

THEY SEARCH FOR DARYA

Under the command of Achmed, first mate of the *Red Witch*, the search parties landed here and there along the beach in the longboats. The Moorish officer hastened to divide his men into groups of six, dispatching them to search the beach, the glade and the edges of the jungles which loomed nearby for any signs of the savage youth or the girl he had so boldly rescued from the very arms of Kâiradine Redbeard.

In truth, Achmed was reluctant to pursue this task. Not only did he consider the expenditure of so much time and energy upon what was, after all, merely another woman—in no wise, according to Achmed's way of thinking, very different from any other young woman—foolish and unwise, but, as well, certain trepidations colored his thinking.

Seventh sons of seventh sons, such as the huge, burly Moorish first mate with the shaven bullet-head, receive eerie and inexplicable premonitions from the Unknown concerning those events yet to come from the womb of unborn time. And, over the long and sanguinary years of his piratical career, Achmed had seen such oninous foreshadowings proven accurate often enough to have learned to trust them.

And the cold worm of fear coiled within the strong and valiant heart of Achmed of El-Cazar. Something whispered to his inner ear that this rash expedition in pursuit of an unimportant, although lovely, young woman, would bring down upon the officers and crewmen of the *Red Witch* a swift and thorough doom.

But such men as Kâiradine Redbeard, called Barbarossa, are both capricious and imperious, and seldom will they brook any interference with the direction of their will or desire. And such was surely the case with the *reis* or captain

On that particular occasion, the Professor, Varak, Yualla, One-Eye, myself and one of the Sotharian warriors whose name I am afraid I have forgotten, but which was something like Thusk, were assigned to sweeping out and mopping up a sector of the caverns which heretofore none of us had seen.

While we were tackling the grime and filth, One-Eye all the while grumbling and griping, for he hated being put to "work fit only for shes," as he put it, another work party of slaves was led past us by a squad of Gorpaks. At the sight of these strangers, little Yualla started and gasped, and Varak, for once, lost his good-humored banter in exchange for a cry of amazement. It was evident that among these other captives they recognized the faces of friends of theirs, fellow-Sotharians they had believed dead in the disaster which had so swiftly overtaken the village.

I paid little attention to their emotion after the first instant. For my heart leaped up with a gasp of wondrous relief—

Among the Sotharians were Jorn the Hunter and Darya, my beloved.

As her eyes met mine she, too, uttered a cry of rapturous joy; then her glorious eyes misted with tears and her face fell in despondency, even as did my own as much the same thought flashed through our minds at the same instant:

I thrilled to the knowledge that she was alive and seemingly unhurt.

But rather would I have known her dead, than to see her here, in the ghastly den of the Sluagghs.

bruised from bumping or scraping our naked bodies against the rough stone walls and sharp protuberances of the caves, and were covered with dust and grime.

Hurok led the way, since he was the only one of us who had ever explored this cavern. But he very soon got lost. The trouble was, I suppose, that feeling your way through the labyrinth of caves in the pitch-black darkness is a lot different from trying to retrace your steps in the light of the torches.

At length he paused, scratching his heavy jaw, small eyes reflecting his bafflement.

"Don't tell me the huge oaf has lost his way," panted Professor Potter testily.

I shrugged, fearing that to be the case, which it more or less was. Hurok came lumbering over to where I stood with Darya, catching my breath. He looked confused.

"Are you lost, Hurok?" I inquired. He slowly shook his huge head.

"Hurok believes that to continue on in this direction will lead the friends of Black Hair to the outer world," said the Neanderthal in his deep, guttural tones.

"Well, then, let's keep going," I suggested. "Surely, by now, all the little Gorpaks in the cavern city are yapping at our heels like a pack of hunting dogs—"

"Black Hair does not understand the hesitation of Hurok," he explained. "Hurok entered the caverns through a hole in the side of the mountain, far up. For Hurok was scaling the mountain and entered the hole in its side to escape the attack of a thakdol."

"In other words, if we keep on going in this direction we will come out on the side of a cliff," I groaned. "Well, that's just dandy! I can just see the whole gang of us, stark naked and worn out, trying to climb down the cliff one by one, with the Gorpaks behind us and the thakdols snapping at our noses."

He nodded heavily. "That thought has also occurred to Hurok," he admitted. "And Hurok suggests that the friends of Black Hair follow this side cavern, which branches off from the way in which Hurok came."

"Do you know where it leads?" inquired the Professor. Hurok solemnly confessed that he did not.

"But the Peaks of Peril are honeycombed with caves and tunnels," he pointed out, "and surely there will be many exits into the daylight world."

"That's probably true," mused Professor Potter, scratching

his nose. "We already know of two others, at least: the door in the wall by which I gained admittance into this disgusting place and the trapdoor atop the cliff wall by which the young lady, here, and her friend Jorn got in. Well, where there are three entrances there will certainly be more. . . ."

"Let us try it then," rumbled Garth who had come near to listen to our conversation.

So we turned aside and entered the cavern that Hurok had advised. It was no less winding and rough than had been the first one we had followed, and at the end of its circuitous path might well lie yet another way out of the hollow mountains. At any rate, our turning off into the side tunnel would possibly confuse the Gorpaks, whom we then thought to be directly behind us, since in their excitement they would probably pass right by the little, narrow entrance to the side tunnel and continue on in the general direction of our flight.

Of course, we had no way of knowing that the shrewd Gorpaks had anticipated that we would do this, since they certainly knew this maze of tunnels better than we, and were planning to ambush us as we emerged from this very tunnel.

Although he has played very little part in the affairs I have been describing to you, One-Eye of course accompanied us. The hulking Apeman had—as we would say in the Upper World—maintained a low profile during the period of our captivity in the cavern city. He ate by himself and slept apart from the others, and seldom if ever communicated with any of us, save in surly grunts. I think that One-Eye was afraid I was going to get my new friends, the Sotharians, to gang up on him in revenge for the brutalities I had experienced at his hands.

Anyway, he kept himself in the rear of things as unobtrusively as was possible under the circumstances, and probably had long planned to get away by himself at the first opportunity.

And this was the first opportunity.

When we turned off into the narrow little side tunnel, One-Eye fell back to the rear and let the rest of us move ahead. As soon as we were gone, the Neanderthal emerged from the side tunnel and continued on down the main tunnel which led to the hole in the face of the cliff.

He thought himself unobserved, doubtless; but in this, One-Eye was seriously mistaken.

Murg the Sotharian, too, had lingered in the rear of our

party, more, I think, from natural cowardice than from any
particular scheme of his own. I believe I have mentioned this
fellow before; he was skinnier and uglier than the other warriors of Sothar, with mean little eyes and an obsequious manner. He was always sucking up to the Gorpaks and cringing
before them and whispering to them in an oily, conspiratorial
way. Instinctively, I disliked and distrusted him, for all that
he was the brother of Garth the High Chief; but never were
two brothers more unlike than these two. Garth was stalwart,
majestic, fearless—a born leader, with the ability to command respect from others. Murg, on the other hand, was wily
and cunning and treacherous, and always looking out for
Murg first and everybody else distinctly second.

He was the sort of person who doesn't have any friends,
only allies and henchmen.

Murg, then, was in a position to observe One-Eye as the
huge Neanderthal slunk out of the tunnel and went waddling
down the main cavern. This action piqued Murg's curiosity,
for he was an inquisitive man, always sticking his nose into
other people's business and meddling in their affairs.

Wondering what One-Eye was up to, Murg yielded to the
temptation to follow, presuming he could always catch up to
the rest of his people should he wish to. So, keeping well to
one side, and making as little noise as possible, he began to
follow One-Eye.

The Apeman of Kor was waddling along at the best speed
his bowed legs and splay feet were able to manage. The trouble was that the others had carried the torches, which meant
that One-Eye had to traverse the tunnel in the dark. And this
meant that he kept bumping into rocky projections and bang-
ing his head on stalactites and things.

It really wasn't very hard for Murg to follow One-Eye. All
he had to do was to keep his ears open and listen for the
thumps when the Neanderthal bumped into something, and
then the growling curse as One-Eye rubbed whichever mem-
ber he had hurt.

Before long, One-Eye saw daylight ahead, and knew that
his journey was nearly over.

Reaching the entrance, he peered cautiously out, looking
around to see if any of those thakdols which Hurok had mentioned were flapping near. None were in sight, so the Apeman
crawled out on the narrow stone ledge which served as the
doorstep of the cave's mouth and looked down.

At the base of the cliff the jungle grew close to the rocky foothills. A narrow ledge zigzagged down for a time, then petered out, but One-Eye could spot footholds and handholds and knew he could descend the cliff without much trouble.

Although a coward and a bully, One-Eye was tough enough. In the jungle world of Zanthodon, weaklings do not survive long enough to grow to One-Eye's age, which I would guess at about forty. While the Neanderthal did not especially like heights, he did not especially fear them. And, with the huge splayed feet and prehensile toes and blunt, thick-fingered hands of his kind, One-Eye could climb as well as a monkey.

But first he concealed himself beside the edge of the entrance. Murg had made more noise than he had intended to, and echoes bounce down caverns. One-Eye didn't know who was following him, but he intended to find out.

So, when Murg poked his nose out, One-Eye pounced!

Chapter 20.

HIDDEN EYES

Tharn of Thandar lifted one hand in the signal for silence, and immediately there ensued a cessation of all activity. His warriors had been striving to pry open the great trapdoor the scouts had discovered at the top of the cliffs, but all their attempts had thus far proved futile. Now, as Komad the scout knelt with his ear close to the rock, Tharn knew that something was amiss.

"What is it, O Komad?" he inquired after a moment.

The leader of the scouts rose to his feet. "Noises from the hollow places below, my Chief," muttered Komad. "The tramp of many marching feet, and the clatter of weapons and accouterments. Someone is approaching the place whereover we stand; therefore, let us fall back to a secure distance and observe what will shortly transpire."

"The suggestion of Komad is wise and prudent," nodded Tharn. And he commanded his warriors to retire some little distance and to remain silent, avoiding any noise that might give the alarm to whoever marched in the cavern below.

Not very long thereafter, the great slab tilted to the pressure of some internal mechanism unseen. And there emerged rapidly into the light of day as curious a troop of men as ever the warriors of Thandar had seen.

They came boiling up out of the space beneath like so many angry hornets whose nest has been disturbed, and they ascended to the top of the cliff from below by means of many bamboo ladders. Uncomprehendingly, the warriors and huntsmen of Thandar stared from where they crouched behind boulders, curious at the hairless, sallow little men with their bandy legs and odd garments and even stranger weapons.

"O Chief, shall we not attack them now, with the advantage of surprise?" whispered Ithar to his monarch. "For whoever these strange little men may be, surely the gomad Darya is their captive, since they rule the hollow places below, into which she must have descended."

Tharn frowned thoughtfully. It went against the rude and simple chivalry of his race to strike from ambush against an unknowing foe, but the counsels of Ithar were wise, and victory alone is the desired end of any conflict. However, as things turned out, it was spared to Tharn of Thandar that he strike the first blow against the Gorpaks, for one of the bandy-legged little grotesques, staring around, spied a hiding Thandarian and squalled, giving the alarm.

He lifted his trident as if to cast it, but it went awry and clattered off a boulder.

In the next instant, a Thandarian arrow pierced the breast of the Gorpak, and the battle was joined.

The man who fell was Vusk, for I was able to identify his corpse later.

From their own hiding place at the cliff's edge, the Barbary pirates stared with amazement as the cliff opened to disgorge a horde of odd-looking little people who promptly charged the Thandarian savages and went down like flies before their arrows and javelins.

"Behold, O Achmed!" whined Tarbu, clutching at the brawny arm of the first mate. "The mountain opens like a door, and forth come devil-men!"

"They are the Djinn!" breathed Achmed, "who dwell in the bosom of Mount Kaf!" All of the superstitions of his race seethed to life in the breast of the Moor, striking fear into his heart as could never a mortal foe, however armed or powerful.

"Let us withdraw from this accursed place, before the stones open beneath our very feet and disgorge demons!" suggested another of the corsairs. Privately, Achmed thought that a very good idea; there was no advantage in going to the assistance of the unknown savages, and there was certainly nothing to be gained in waiting here for the devil-men to destroy the primitives and then come after the pirates.

So he gave quick orders, and in less time than it would take me to describe the scene, the Barbary corsairs clambered back down the improvised log ladders and concealed themselves within the edges of the jungle, the better to observe what transpired.

It soon became obvious that the Gorpaks were getting the worst of the fight. Not only were the Cro-Magnon savages taller and stronger, but they were much better fighting men than the Gorpaks, with much more experience in war.

Hitherto, the Gorpaks had done little more than lay traps in the jungle for passing men or women, and strutted and preened themselves before the listless cavern folk. There had never been a mutiny of the slaves of the cavern city until Garth and I led the one I have described.

The fact of the matter was, the Gorpaks had never been in a real battle before and they didn't know what to do. They stood, shouting orders at the Thandarians, shrilling abuse, waving their arms, instead of taking cover. So, of course, they fell in droves to the arrows and spears hurled against them. And when it finally dawned on the Gorpaks that they were not exactly winning this thing, they tried to go back down into the caverns again, but were prevented from effecting their retreat by the pressure of more Gorpaks climbing up from below. That is, by this time Lutho had arrived with the reinforcements, and they were boiling up out of the exit to stand bewilderedly, finding themselves in the midst of a battle.

Except that it really wasn't a battle at all, but very quickly became a full-fledged massacre.

It would have pleased me mightily, could I have been there to see it. Simpering little Vusk fell to an arrow in the throat, and the obsequious Sunth took a Thandarian spear in the heart, and even the villainous little brute whom the Professor had surprised in the act of whipping a child of the caverns died in the holocaust.

Tridents make clumsy weapons, pitted against spears.

And whips are of even less use against arrows.

It was all over very quickly. Captain Lutho managed to escape by jumping off the edge of the cliff. We found his body later at the base, where he had landed on some rocks, which split his skull open like an eggshell.

It certainly wasn't Lutho's day, was it?

As the gigantic drunth came thundering down upon Xask, the Zarian did the only thing that occurred to him. Since he had no other weapon at hand save the automatic pistol which he had taken from me, he plucked it out and pointed it at the dinosaur, hoping against hope to somehow evoke the power of the so-called thunder-weapon.

Fortune was with Xask in that hour, despite her neglect of him in recent days. By pure chance his finger slid into the trigger guard and tightened about the trigger. A deafening retort sounded. The noise made Xask jump; it also so startled Fumio that he fell out of his tree and landed with a bruising thump in a thick thornbush.

The vast size of the armored stegosaurus loomed above Xask like a moving mountain. The monster halted—faltered—then, with a crash that shook the earth, it toppled over on its side and lay, kicking enormous feet and flexing and unflexing its long, blade-edged tail.

Xask was coughing to clear his head of the stench of gunpowder. He shook his head to stop the ringing in his ears, and stared wonderingly down at the smoking barrel of the .45.

Then he strolled around the body of the drunth, kicking it in the side from time to time, but carefully avoiding the lashing tail, which could snap his spine like a twig.

He found a black, sooty-edged hole at the base of the throat of the drunth, which must have been caused by the thunder-weapon. It mystified Xask that so tiny a wound could have brought down so mighty a monster, and, in fact, it mystifies me, for in my time I have bounced a bullet or two off a dinosaur, to no effect at all.

The Professor has a Theory—(the Professor *always* has a Theory)—that Xask's bullet must have entered the dinosaur's carcass through the soft flesh of the throat and caught it directly in the spinal cord, shattering that vital chain of vertebrae and causing it instant paralysis, rather than death. I don't know, neither did Xask, but anyway his slug stopped the stegosaurus cold.

Eventually, he strolled over and pried Fumio out of the thornbush. Once Fumio had plucked out thorns from the more tender parts of his anatomy, and got a good look at the body of the drunth, he fell on his face and began kissing the feet of Xask.

Fumio knew a god when he saw one. Only a god could have felled a monster like that with a bolt from the blue.

Xask permitted Fumio to fawn on him for a time, then he commanded his new slave to get to his feet and accompany him through the jungle. Fumio was happy enough to do as his god ordered. Surely, armed with the thunders of the firmament, Xask could protect Fumio from the perils of the wild, the vengeance of Tharn, the cruelty of One-Eye and just about anything else.

Which is about all we could possibly hope for from the gods.

As the battle on the cliff top came to its eventual end, there were other eyes watching from a place of hidden concealment besides those of the Barbary pirates. And these were the eyes of Xask and Fumio, who had arrived on the scene just after the corsairs had concealed themselves in the jungle.

Xask watched thoughtfully as the Thandarian savages finished off the last of the Gorpaks. He wondered, I suppose, what in the world was going on, but then Xask had never before seen any Gorpaks, and neither had he ever seen the Barbary pirates. This world of Zanthodon was proving a more remarkable place than even Xask had ever guessed, and was crowded with strange peoples of whose very existence he had gone ignorant all his days.

As was always the case with men like Xask, his cold and cunning brain went instantly to work calculating how this new information could be bent to serve his best interests.

As for Fumio, he wasn't thinking about anything much; he wasn't even watching the end of the battle. True, Tharn was there, and Fumio would have been very fearful and wary of Tharn a few hours before, for, after all, he had attempted to rape the daughter of Tharn, which was great and good reason for Fumio to feel fear.

But he didn't. After all, his god was at his side, and there at the waist of his god was the thunder-weapon.

And he felt very safe and secure, did Fumio.

It was about the same time that the rest of us arrived on the scene. The wandering tunnel had carried us to the door in the cliff, through which the Professor had first entered the cavern city, and once we found the secret of the mechanism that triggered the counterweights, we opened it and emerged into the light of day.

The first thing we saw was Lutho's crushed corpse amid the rocks.

Then we looked up and saw the Thandarian host atop the cliffs, and they looked down and saw us.

Of course, they didn't know who the host of Sotharian warriors were, but it didn't much matter to Tharn. For among the throng of newcomers he recognized me, the old Professor and Jorn the Hunter, to say nothing of Hurok of Kor.

And his daughter Darya, of course. She was standing very close to me and I had my arm around her shoulders. As soon as I saw Tharn of Thandar, I flushed crimson and took my hand away. After all, you will recall, Darya and I were both nude. And even Stone Age fathers have notions of propriety.

Raising a halloo, the Thandarians came swarming down the cliff, and a moment later Tharn seized his daughter up and crushed her slender body in his embrace and gave her a kiss that probably made her toes curl.

The next instant he slapped me approvingly on the shoulder, nearly knocking me down, and crushed my hand in his in a grateful handshake that very nearly reduced my knuckles to powder.

And it was all over.

Or so, at the time, we thought. . . .

Part Five

VICTORY IN ZANTHODON

Chapter 21.

THE BOND OF FRIENDSHIP

Garth and the men and women of Sothar had withdrawn a little ways as the Thandarians had begun their descent from the cliff top and now stood in a close group, wary and watchful. Of course, they did not know the men of Thandar to be friendly, and of course the men of Thandar actually weren't; in Zanthodon, the hand of every man and nation is pitted against every other, and a stranger is considered to be a foe until his actions prove him a friend.

Noticing the constraint of the Sotharians, I beckoned Garth forward and led him to where Tharn stood, talking with his daughter. Seeing us, he gently put her aside, for he had men's work to do.

"O Tharn, High Chief of the warriors of Thandar," I said in the formal diction of their language, "let me make known to you my friend and ally, Garth, High Chief of the warriors of Sothar. It is the dearest wish of Eric Carstairs that the people of Thandar should be friends with the people of Sothar."

Garth and Tharn looked each other over from head to toe and probably approved of what they saw—they were, after all, nearly as much alike as cousins, both being tall, majestic men in their full prime, magnificent of physique, strong and manly of visage.

Then Tharn reached out his hand.

"The wish of Eric Carstairs is likewise the wish of Tharn," he said with simple dignity. "Greetings and peace to my brother, the Omad of Sothar, if that he come in peace."

"In peace we meet, Omad of Thandar, and in peace we shall part," said Garth, seizing the hand of Tharn. For a moment the two stood eye to eye, maintaining their aloof dignity.

Then they grinned at each other, and the ice was broken.

Erelong, the Thandarians were divesting themselves of some of their spare clothing, so that the men of Sothar could wrap a bit of fur about their loins and the women could also cover themselves. Grateful for at least one of the amenities of civilization, I adjusted about my loins a scrap of fur about the size of a ladies' handkerchief, which I bound about my waist with a piece of thong.

It wasn't much, but it felt good to be "dressed."

The Professor looked remarkably funny in his little fur apron, with his bony ribs and skinny legs bare to the view. But through all of our adventures he had held onto his pince-nez glasses, and his absurd sun helmet; now, these two items lent him a dignity that black tie formal wear could not have given.*

We drank water and rested and ate some of the stores of the Thandarians, and told of our adventures. The Thandarians looked grim as they learned of the horrors we had witnessed in the cavern city, and were amazed to learn of the Sluagghs, of whose very existence they had been happily ignorant.

Soon the two bands of warriors began constructing weapons so that the men of Sothar might arm themselves. Sharp blades trimmed saplings into spears and whittled crude but serviceable arrows, while the women worked at fashioning bows and slings. Stone axes were the easiest to make, for the foot of the cliffs was littered with bits of broken or crumbling rock.

Once armed, the combined host numbered a mighty force. The two groups of Sotharians must have totaled in excess of fifty, most of them grown men and warriors, but some of them women, old men and young children. Even these could fight, of course, for in the Underground World all are taught to defend themselves as a matter of course. There are few noncombatants in Zanthodon.

As for the Thandarians, they numbered about fifty warriors as well, perhaps a trifle more, and their numbers had now been augmented by the addition of Hurok, the Professor, Jorn, Darya and myself. We now added up to quite a large army, as armies go in the Stone Age.

---

* He had also hung onto his little black notebook and pen, which he now carried under his helmet. I guess he wouldn't have felt like a scientist if he had been unable to take notes.

And we felt confident that we could invade the cavern city, destroy the Gorpaks, slaughter the vampiric leeches and set free the listless cavern folk—although what they would do with their freedom I could not imagine, so broken and cowed had they become under generations of slavery to their bandy-legged little masters.

First, however, we must sleep. I could not recall just how long it had been since I last enjoyed a good sleep, and I ached in every muscle. With the freshest of us standing guard against any attack by Gorpaks or beasts, the rest of us fell into a deep and refreshing slumber.

As for the Barbary pirates, they were in a quandary, if not indeed a dilemma. Achmed and his corsairs could clearly identify Darya, for they had been present at the time when Kâiradine Redbeard had borne the jungle girl aboard his vessel, the *Red Witch*. But she was in the very midst of her people, and they dared not attack; neither, recalling the vicious temper of their Captain, did they dare not attack.

It was a pretty problem! Had Darya been among the warriors of Thandar alone, the pirates might well have gambled on an assault, counting on the advantage of surprise and on the edge of technological superiority their weapons gave them. After all, cutlasses and scimitars of whetted steel are more efficient than homemade arrows, spears and stone axes.

The trouble was, simply, the men of Sothar, whose force had now joined with the Thandarians, more than doubling their number. It would have been rash and foolhardy to the point of being suicidal had Achmed attempted to fight so huge a host with his little band.

"Mayhap, O Achmed, we should return to the ship to summon our brethren to our aid?" Kemal hissed in the ear of his commander.

"Dog of a Turk, has it not occurred to you that during our absence from the scene, on such a mission as you describe, the wench may well depart with her kinsmen?" replied the Moor scornfully.

The Turk tugged on his superb mustachios as if thereby to stimulate the processes of his intellect.

"There is sense and reason in the words of Achmed," Kemal admitted. "Let us, rather, send back only part of our number. . . ."

"And thereby weaken our strength so that, if it should come to a battle, we should surely all be slain? By the beard of the prophet, dog, leave the thinking to one who possesses the wits required, and hold your tongue before I slit it with my dagger!"

Grumbling, Kemal of Istamboul lapsed into moody silence.

Achmed chewed on his lower lip, peering out between the leaves of the thickly grown bush behind which he crouched. Bluff and bluster all he would, he had no better ideas to offer than those already proposed by Kemal. But he could hardly admit that without losing face in the eyes of the ruffians he commanded.

What do you do when there really isn't anything you can do?

Perhaps you have to take a dangerous chance....

Achmed mumbled a prayer to his god, but under his breath. The only possibility which occurred to him was to wait and see what transpired next. If the savages, upon awakening, began to march away through the jungles, he supposed that he would have to risk all on the uncertain outcome of an ambush.

What he was really hoping for was that Darya should stray away from the host of warriors, or should for some reason be left alone, or among only a few of her people.

Well, for the moment the Moorish first mate determined to do nothing at all. He would simply wait and see what happened next.

It wasn't the most bold and daring plan in the world, he glumly realized, but it was better than nothing.

We awoke, rested and refreshed. I have always tried to get my eight hours in the sack, no matter where I was or what was happening around me. Seldom have I slept so deeply as when the world was exploding about my ears; I remember sleeping like an innocent babe through part of one of those minor Near Eastern wars, with the Arabs and the Israelis popping away at each other over my head.

Of course, in Zanthodon it is impossible to ascertain exactly when eight hours have passed, unless you just sit there and count "one-thousand-one, one-thousand-two," and so on, until you have measured eight hours by. Of course, that way you wouldn't get any sleep at all, but what the hell, at least you'd know just how long you *didn't* sleep.

We had breakfast. Tharn's hunters had brought down a brace of zomaks, which the women of both tribes defeathered and broiled on spits over shallow fire pits. Zomaks are the

nearest things Zanthodon can boast of comparable to birds.
They are surely the strangest birds you ever saw, with scaly
tails and beaks filled with sharp, nasty little teeth. Professor
Potter calls them "archaeopteryx," and says they are the ancestors of birds.

Well, maybe so, but they sure don't taste as good as
chicken!

Not to be outdone by the feats of the Thandarian hunters,
the huntsmen of Sothar went into the jungle and emerged after a time with several plump uld. The uld are peculiar little
critters. They resemble slim, long-legged pigs with tapering
muzzles instead of snouts, and they sport a rough coat of
short fur. The Professor identifies them as "eohippus," and
tells me they are the ancestors of the horse. Maybe so. . . .

Between pseudo-bird and proto-horse we made a fair meal,
I must admit. With more than a hundred mouths to feed, the
rations didn't stretch too well, but we filled up on fruits and
nuts and berries, wherewith this part of the jungle country
abounded.

I believe I have said very little about the fruits of Zanthodon in these narratives. That is not because there were none,
for there were plenty. It is because the Cro-Magnon tribes
scorn the eating of fruit, which they regard as fit only for
children and old women. *Meat* is the thing a Cro-Magnon
craves; everything else is mere filler. As a filet mignon man
myself, I can appreciate their feelings; but when it comes to
going into battle with a tummy only half-filled, or chomping
down some vegetarian goodies, I will chose the latter every
time.

There is not much to say about the fruits of Zanthodon.
For one thing, the Cro-Magnons have no names for different
kinds of fruit, they lump everything together under one heading: *gooma*. It is a rather derogatory word, and may be
translated roughly as "babyfood." One kind of gooma looks
and tastes quite like a mango, another resembles a cross between bananas and breadfruit. There is another variety resembling coconuts, but soft and hairless of shell.

It all tasted pretty good to me, but the men of Thandar
and of Sothar made faces as they gulped down what they regarded as disgusting, messy stuff.

It takes all kinds, I guess.

When we were through with our meal, we took up our
weapons and made ourselves ready for the expedition down

into the caverns. The women and children of the Sotharians we would leave behind, together with the few old people, such as the old wise man, Coph. I prevailed upon the Professor and Darya to remain with them, overriding their protests.

"It's a job for younger and more vigorous men than yourself, Doc," I said honestly. "Don't be offended, but you'd really be in the way."

He sniffed, giving me a frosty glare. But I know he understood.

I made my farewells to Darya. They were rather formal ones, for I had not yet declared myself as a contender for her hand. We did not stand close, or kiss, or even touch. But our eyes, as the saying has it, spoke volumes. Volumes of love poems, that is.

"Fare you well, chief's daughter," I said. "May the Unseen Ones have you in their keeping."*

"Fare you well, chieftain," she said simply. I turned away.

"Eric Carstairs!" she called after me. I turned to look at her again.

Her voice was very low, as if choked by some emotion whose name and nature I scarcely dared hope I knew.

"Yes?"

"Come back safely . . . to me!"

My heart surged within me; all at once I was sixteen years old again, and just got a valentine from the Raquel Welch of my high school. I felt buoyant, filled with absurd self-confidence. I smiled, nodded, waved my hand and turned away.

We marched for the ladders.

And behind us, from the shelter of the bushes, Achmed of the Barbary pirates smiled a cold, cruel, cunning smile as his eyes rested on Darya of Thandar. . . .

---

* The Unseen Ones are about as close as the Cro-Magnon tribes come to conceiving of gods. They are beneficent, protective spirits. Sometimes the Cro-Magnons speak of them as almost gods, or at least as powerful spiritual entities; at other times, they seem to think of them as the ghosts of their ancestors. There is no formal worship given.

Chapter 22.

INTO THE CAVERNS

Other eyes were also watching from places of concealment. Xask and Fumio crouched behind the bole of a tall Jurassic conifer, watching as we ascended the cliffs. And the eyes of Xask were narrowed in concentration.

He had once fired the automatic, but he really did not understand how it worked or the extent and limitation of its powers. For that he needed the cooperation of Eric Carstairs. And he was well aware that Eric Carstairs would not willingly cooperate. He needed some sort of leverage over the man whose mind bore the information he was determined to possess. . . .

As for Fumio, his eyes were turned adoringly upon his god. You must understand the reasons for Fumio's rapid and thorough conversion to Xaskianity. The outlawed Thandarian chieftain had never chanced to be present on any of those occasions when I had fired the .45. He had heard rumors of the "thunder-weapon," as both the Cro-Magnons and the Neanderthals called my gun, but had paid little attention.

Fumio was rotten to the core, an arrogant, sneering bully and a lily-livered coward—by my personal standards, at least. A strong, brave man does not try to rape a defenseless girl. Alone and lost and friendless in the trackless jungles, Fumio would probably have survived—after a fashion—but would not have made a very good job of it.

Then along came Xask.

Fumio was well aware that he was not very intelligent. He was handsome, or had been before Jorn broke his nose; and he was superbly muscular, a good hunter and a good warrior. But he had no smarts.

Xask was very smart. He was one of the most intelligent and crafty devils I have ever known. Glib and articulate, a

159

born con man, Xask could have talked his way out from between the very jaws of a hungry sabertooth tiger.

Not being very intelligent, Fumio admired and envied those who were. And Xask certainly was.

Not being very confident of himself, after the fiasco he had made of things recently, Fumio respected and envied those who were. And Xask was supremely confident.

Put all of that together, then remember that Fumio had looked on as Xask felled a rampaging stegosaurus with a bolt of lightning. The drunth, as the Cro-Magnons call the stegosaurus, is a large and very fearsome reptile. Unlike many of its kind, it is a carnivore. Even the boldest and bravest of the warriors of Thandar will take to their heels if a drunth appears on the scene. And Xask had toppled one as easy as pie.

Hence Fumio's conversion to the worship of Xask.

And Xask didn't at all mind being worshipped. . . .

We entered the caverns beneath the hollow mountains by two different routes. Half of our host clambered up the ladders and went down into the underground city by means of the great trapdoor atop the cliffs. The other half marched through the door in the cliff wall which we had left ajar, wedging one of the burnt-out torches between the door and the jamb so as to block the mechanism.

It was by this route that I and my warriors entered the caverns. Yes, when Darya hailed me as "chieftain," she was only giving me my due. For Tharn and Garth, in conference, had both decided to reward me for my services by creating me a chieftain in the temporarily combined tribes. I felt quite flattered.

Also, quite put-upon. For a Cro-Magnon chieftain gets to pick and choose his own warriors, and just about everybody clamored to serve under me. By triggering the slave revolt and leading the successful escape out of the cavern city, I had built quite a reputation for myself.

I chose, in the end, Varak of the Sotharians, Hurok of Kor, Jorn the Hunter and seven other of the warriors of the combined tribes. I would have liked to have had old Komad on my combat team, but he was already a chieftain on his own.

We were determined to clean out the nest of human and nonhuman filth that dwelt beneath the Peaks of Peril. The Gorpaks would have to be our first concern, because they stood in our path directly. But I had vowed in my heart to eradicate the Sluagghs from Zonthodon if it took a thousand years. We were fully aware of the dangers we faced: but the Sluagghs had to be destroyed. I might never leave Zanthodon and return to the Upper World again, but either way I would never be able to enjoy a night of peaceful sleep again, knowing that the horrible vampire leeches were breeding down there in the filth and slime of their black burrows.

Incidentally, we were by now aware that a few of us were missing. I was not surprised to learn that One-Eye had seized the opportunity to run off, and was heartily glad to be rid of the fellow. But the men and women of Sothar were puzzled to find that Murg had vanished.

Well, these were mysteries to be cleared up later, and we simply left it to that. Right now, we had more important work to do.

The warriors constructed torches and set them alight with their flints and began to file into the caverns again. Leaving the women of Sothar behind, together with such noncombatants as Darya and the Professor, the rest of us entered the caverns and got about our grisly business. Gorpak reinforcements were gathered by this time, and soon we found the entrance into the cavern city itself blocked by a barricade. We eliminated the barrier through the simple expedient of setting it afire; when the Gorpaks fled squealing, we scattered the burning wreckage with the tips of our spears, and pressed on.

The Gorpaks had never been invaded before, and could hardly believe that this was happening. Gorpak after Gorpak took a stand before us, shrilly ordering us to throw down our weapons and surrender, "in the name of the Lords." We didn't waste time talking but put an arrow through such as these and kept on going. Whenever they tried to make a fight of it, we cut them to pieces. The pity of it was, the little creatures didn't really know how to fight and never even had a chance. It was ugly business, but it had to be done.

While the men of Thandar went about their work with grim efficiency, not really enjoying the slaughter, the warriors of Sothar were not so squeamish. Not a one of them there was that had not suffered at the hands of the Gorpaks, or who had been forced to stand helplessly by as Gorpaks subjected their mates and children to indignities I do not care to describe. So the men of Sothar cut the Gorpaks down with savage relish, nor could I find it in my heart to blame them overmuch.

One of the last to die was Queb, the ancient shaman of the Gorpaks. When we had penetrated to the very entrance to the Chamber of Feasting, he stood in our way, waving his skinny arms, clanking his beads and amulets, shaking his gourd rattles.

We were reluctant to kill the old man in cold blood, for he was not armed. Fortunately, Queb solved that problem for us by charging our line, shrilling imprecations. Automatically, the warriors raised their spears to fend him off, but in his frenzy the old witch doctor impaled himself on the spears and died quickly.

In retrospect, I realize that we had utterly no choice. All of the warriors who marched with us were of the same mind, and knew that we had no alternative but to invade the cavern city of the Gorpaks, if only to make sure that the rest of their captives and slaves were set free and the last of the Gorpaks wiped out.

Privately, I determined to exterminate the Sluagghs like the unholy vermin they were. None of us who had undergone the ordeal in the hollow mountains really wanted to go down there again. That was only natural and human of us; but we were also men. And men sometimes have to do things they don't really want to, or abandon honor and manhood.

The price of courage is very high. No hero myself, I know just how expensive bravery is. You have to swallow your fear, ignore your sweating palms and the queasiness in the pit of your stomach, and put a bold face on things. Or stop calling yourself a man. . . .

I am a man.

With Queb disposed of, we entered the Cavern of Feasting without further opposition, and pried up the great slab in the floor. All of us had brought with us torches which would burn brightly, so we knew we had little or nothing to fear from the monster leeches, so long as we did not look into their multiple eyes and thus permit them to gain the mastery of our minds.

We planned to kill them all, even the young. The Sluagghs were too dreadful a peril to allow them to continue their existence; they were the only, and the best, argument for genocide I have ever heard. They truly had no right to live, and I was convinced they must all be sought out and slaughtered.

The men of Thandar did not understand my feelings on

this, but the men of Sothar were of the same mind. And so we killed them, holding high the blazing torches, spearing them to death as they flopped and wriggled on their beds of slime. They died quite easily, one spear thrust did it. You punctured their clammy hides and out spewed a vile, stinking black fluid that could only have been old, putrid human blood.

We slew them in a cold, hating fury. And then we went after the ones that had slithered away into the deeper burrows. It was a dirty, disgusting job, wading into those black sewers, murdering the slimy monsters in the fetid gloom, but it had to be done.

In the end we found their nests, tunneled far under the floor of the cavern. The young of the Sluagghs were like pale, wet grubs, and they were the size of human babies. Like infants, they squealed and mewed as they died.

I leaned against the wall and lost my breakfast in wracking, painful spasms. Not one of the warriors around me thought any the less of my courage or manhood for this. More than a few had vomited before me, and others were soon to follow us. The stench of the nests was horrible beyond belief.

I say little of this episode. It is not one of the things I have done that I am proud of. It was a dirty job, but it had to be done, and we did it. But it was not something you would want to remember afterwards.

When we came out, after it was all over, we were sick from the smell and covered with reeking filth, and trembling with nervous reaction. We washed ourselves off in one of the conduits that bore cold water from springs within the mountain through the cavern city for the purpose of sanitation.

Even after washing, we still felt unclean. And we all wished later that we could have washed our memories as we had washed our bodies. For the hideous experience lived in our dreams and especially in our nightmares for a long while afterward.

But at least it was over, and we had rid the world of the Sluagghs for all time.

And *that* was a job well worth doing!

Chapter 23.

FUMIO REAPPEARS

Once the warriors of Thandar and Sothar had vanished from view within the hollow cliff, Xask and Fumio were free to act. Darya, Professor Potter, the old wise man, Coph, and the women and children of the Sotharian tribe were alone in the clearing, guarded only by a small number of warriors who had sustained minor injuries during their adventures which, while not incapacitating them, rendered them temporarily unfit for such exertions as the war against the Gorpaks.

Whispering conspiratorially together, the two villains laid their plans.

Moments later, Fumio emerged from the underbrush and walked boldly up to the guards. Those among them who were men of Thandar were astonished to see him alive, for it was thought that he had either long since perished in the jungle or had been carried off a captive of the Apemen to Kor. But here he was, alive and well, strolling casually into the encampment as if assured of a friendly greeting and a hospitable welcome.

"Does the chieftain Fumio yet live, then?" one of the huntsmen of Thandar, a fine-looking fellow named Ragor, wondered.

Fumio spread his hands with an easy smile.

"As Ragor sees, fortune has smiled on Fumio and he has braved the dangers of the wild to rejoin his countrymen," he said smoothly.

"Erdon perceives that someone has broken the nose of the chieftain Fumio," remarked another Thandarian warrior.

Fumio lost a little of his composure; for a moment an ugly glint showed in his eyes. Then he smiled easily again, with a wordless shrug.

By this time he had come very near to where the two guards stood. He did not seem to be armed.

As for Darya, she was so amazed at this sudden and unexpected reappearance of one she thought long dead that she was, literally, speechless. Since Jorn the Hunter had interrupted Fumio in the act of attempting to rape her, knocked him down and chased him away, she had long ago dismissed the very existence of her false-hearted former suitor from her mind. To find him turning up now, bold as brass, as if nothing had chanced to occur between them, momentarily robbed her of the ability of speech. She could hardly believe her eyes.

Perhaps I should explain at this point that while Jorn and Darya had informed the Omad of Thandar of the treachery of Fumio, this was a matter of private information and had not been spread throughout the ranks of the men of Thandar. It might have been wiser of Tharn had he informed his warriors of the villainies of the deposed and outlawed chieftain, but as he assumed Fumio to be dead, there seemed no reason for the event to be made a topic of general knowledge.

Had he chosen to do otherwise, of course, this history would have taken a very different turn. . . .

Professor Potter was speechless with amazement, too, but recovered the use of his tongue before Fumio had quite entered the encampment. He leveled a shaking and accusatory finger at the smiling villain.

"Great Galileo, but that's the rogue who struck me down with a cowardly blow from behind and was trying to assault the young lady here before Jorn pounced on him, ruined his handsome face and drove him off in scorn!" he shrilled, red-faced with outrage.

Instantly, Ragor and Erdon snapped to attention, lifting their weapons to readiness. But it was already too late for such measures, for Fumio was among them by that time. He seized the still speechless Darya and from the cover of the furs which clothed his loins, whipped out a sharp flint knife, whose keen edge he placed at the base of Darya's throat.

"Lay down your weapons, or my blade will drink the life of the gomad Darya," he snarled. Stony-faced, the two warriors let their spears fall to the sward.

"Do not any of the rest of you move or attempt to interfere with us," warned Fumio. "Come, woman!" he commanded Darya, giving her arm a vicious twist. Unresistingly, the girl rose to her feet and accompanied him as he forced her from the encampment and the protection of her friends.

"The old man, too," called Xask from the edge of the trees. Speechless with fury and outrage, the Professor was made to follow after them, for he dared not protest lest the Princess of Thandar be made to suffer for his recalcitrance.

Obviously, it had occurred to the wily Xask that, even if Eric Carstairs was not available to teach the secrets of the thunder-weapon, the old man who had accompanied him into the world of Zanthodon might well be made to do so.

"Let none of you dare follow us, on peril to the life of your Princess," warned Xask.

Bitterly, and with grim forebodings, the men of Thandar and Sothar stood helplessly as the two captives were led away into the jungles.

"What will we say to Eric Carstairs, when he returns out of the hollow mountains?" groaned Erdon to his companions. "His heart will be filled with wrath when he discovers that we, who were charged with the protection of their safety, have permitted the old man, his friend and fellow countryman, and the gomad Darya to be taken from our midst. . . ."

"More to the point," growled a burly warrior named Warza, "how will we explain it to the Omad Tharn when he asks us what has become of his beloved daughter?"

"Far better than we pursue them with stealth and in secret, even if we fall in battle against those men than that we stand idly here, doing nothing," said one of the Sotharians, a fine chap called Parthon. "For the High Chief of my people, as well, will deal harshly with those who betrayed the trust which reposed in them. For it was Eric Carstairs who freed us from the slave pens, and led us forth out of the mountains; and it does not take a wise man to have noticed that Eric Carstairs looks with warmth upon the beautiful gomad of Thandar, and would win her for his mate."

"What shall we do?" queried Coph. "If the warriors pursue the two men into the jungle, they will leave defenseless the women and children of Sothar."

At that word, Nian, the mate of Garth, and young Yualla, her daughter, spoke up indignantly.

"Are the women of Sothar so helpless that they cannot defend themselves?" demanded Nian, her splendid eyes flashing. "Are our bowels weak with fear at the thought of holding axe or spear or bow?"

"Let the warriors enter the jungles, and do all that can be done to set our friends free of their cowardly captors," cried Yualla fiercely. "And in their absence, the women and children and the old people of Sothar will protect themselves with vigilance and courage—go!"

Without a word the nine warriors left behind to guard the encampment seized up their weapons and vanished into the edge of the jungle without a backward glance.

Having washed the filth and slime of the burrows from my body, I was resting near the conduit when my lieutenants, Jorn and Varak, came up to me, saluting.

"All has been accomplished as you desired, my chieftain," said the young Hunter. "The slave pens of the Gorpaks have given up their captives, who even now are being fed and their hurts tended. But we have been followed hence by these whom my chieftain sees at our heels. . . ."

He gestured, rather helplessly. I turned to see a number of the naked cavern folk lurking timidly at the entrance to this particular corridor. They seemed shy and confused, and furtively averted their eyes from the Gorpak corpse or two which lay about the floor. The dead Gorpaks seemed to shock them, and more than a few looked faintly scandalized.

I groaned; sooner or later, someone must deal with the folk of the caverns. It was just that, right then, I didn't quite feel up to it. But there was nobody else around to do the job but me.

During our excursion into the cavern city, the listless ones had stayed well out of our way. Although it must have scared the wits out of them to see people actually fighting and killing the precious Gorpaks, they were too timid and too lacking in any of the powers of will or decision to oppose us or even get in our path. Nor did they come to the aid of the Gorpaks. They just ran away and hid, although many of them tried to go about their ordinary routines and tasks as if the battle weren't roaring and rampaging all around them.

I got to my feet and went over to where they huddled. They eyed me shyly; I looked them over and saw that they were not so much fearful as perplexed. Fear was something they had lived with all their lives—fear of the Gorpaks, fear of the whips, fear of the Sluagghs. I could understand that fear; by now it was bred into them. They woke with it, slept with it, ate it with lunch, copulated (joylessly) with it ever at their side, and died with it near at hand.

But perplexity was something new to their experience. Their lives had been things of orderly routine up until now. Everything they did they had been told to do. They had never felt doubt, for every factor in their miserable, pallid lives was laid out and prescribed by the Gorpaks. And now the Gorpaks were dead, all of them.

They didn't know what to do. By invading the sanctity of the subterranean realm of the Sluagghs, by decimating the Gorpaks, we had turned their entire orderly little world upside down and shaken it briskly. For such as the zombie-like cavern folk, the universe itself had been transformed into a new and mysterious system, whose laws and regulations they did not comprehend.

I tried explaining to them what had occurred, but I could see from their faces that it was no good. Too many shocks, too many new things, and they would go into catatonia or something.

In the end, I did it the simple way. The way I knew they would understand.

"Attention!" I barked in my best parade-ground voice. "The Gorpaks have sinned against the Lords. The Lords have decreed the destruction of the Gorpaks. The Lords have decreed that we, the Ones-Who-Cover-Their-Bodies-and-Bear-Weapons, shall replace the Gorpaks. We are your masters now, and you shall obey us in all things. Is that understood?"

One of the males took it upon himself to nod tentatively. Since all I was getting from the rest of the lot was glaze-eyed, slack-jawed mystification, I singled this particular fellow out of the crowd.

"You!" I snapped, pointing. "What are you called?"

"The Gorpaks always called me Hoom, master," he said timidly.

I nodded importantly. "Very well, Hoom. From this moment you are appointed to the following tasks. You will see to it that all of the rest of your people are instructed in what I have just told you about the sin of the Gorpaks, their destruction, and ourselves being appointed by the Lords to be your new masters. Do you understand?"

He nodded hesitantly. "I *think* so, master."

"Very good! Now, here are further orders for you all. They are to be obeyed to the letter, even when we, your masters, are not present to enforce them. Food is to be prepared as food has always been prepared, and gathered as food has always been gathered. Only from now on it is your people, Hoom, who shall see to the preparing of the meals and their distribution, and the tending of the fires. For the Gorpaks no longer are here to perform these tasks. And we, your new masters, will be away for some time on business of the Lords."

I thought for a minute, then added:

"From those storerooms where the clothing of the Gorpaks is kept, you and your people will fashion new garments for yourselves. With these garments, you will cover your loins, even as your masters cover theirs. This rule is to include your mates as well as yourselves. This is a particular sign of the favor you now enjoy under your new masters, and a sign that you have won favor in the eyes of the Lords—"

He blanched and his lips trembled. And I suddenly realized that, in the peculiar parlance of the cavern city, the favor of the Lords is to permit such as Hoom to supply them the nutriment of their life blood. Hastily, I covered myself.

"As another sign of the favor of the Lords, you and all of your people are permanently excused from serving the Lords at the Feastings," I proclaimed.

Well, it would have done your heart good to have seen their faces. Cowed and broken in spirit as they were, these men were still men and the women still women. Eyes brightened in disbelief, and bowed shoulders straightened a little. I saw one mother clutch her young daughter to her and—actually, although tremulously—*smile*.

"The Lords have gone away for a long time. They will still be gone many, many wakes and sleeps after you and your people have died of old age, and your children have grown to adulthood. In fact, the Lords will never return again."

. That seemed to clinch it. Hoom stood taller than I had yet seen one of the cavern people stand, and there was something in his eyes I had never before seen.

"It is . . . true, master, what you say?" he whispered—and instantly cringed, anticipating that I would strike him for daring to doubt the truth of my words.

Instead, I smiled. And looked him straight in the eye.

"It is true, Hoom. I swear it by the Lords themselves. They have all gone away to a far, far place. And from that far place they will never, never return. All of this city they entrust to you and your people, through us, your new masters. But we are soon going away ourselves, and you and those whom you select to give the orders must now tend to the needs of the city without recourse to your masters. Go, now, and tell your people what I have said."

And he went, slowly and hesitantly, but with his back straight and his head up, followed by the others, who cast us timid backward glances, whispering among themselves, still not quite able to believe the miracle of their freedom.

I felt very tired.

I also felt like crying.

Chapter 24.

A TIMELY INTERRUPTION

As Xask and Fumio led Darya through the brush, the jungle girl was thinking furiously to herself. To be so briefly reunited with her friend, Eric Carstairs, for whom certain strange feelings were burgeoning within her breast—feelings she could not quite put a name to—and, for an even briefer span of time, to be united again with her mighty sire and her fellow countrymen was too cruel to be endured without protest and revolt.

There seemed little that the savage girl could do to fight her captors. While Xask was small and slender and no fighting man from the look of his smooth face and puny limbs, Fumio was a mighty warrior and possessed twice the strength of her slim, lithe body. But Darya was coldly determined not to yield supinely to her present circumstances. The problem was—what could she do to circumvent them?

I have said it before but I will repeat it once again: the women of the Cro-Magnon tribes were no soft, pampered playthings. Many of them could run and hunt and fight nearly as well as a man. Life in this primitive subterranean world was hard and cruel; danger lay to every side in the form of savage beasts, hostile tribes, and nature herself, with all her storms and famines, earthquakes and pestilences.

To survive in so inhospitable an environment, even the children must acquire strength, agility, cool nerves and fighting skills. All of these faculties Darya possessed in abundance, as well as intelligence and patience and courage.

They had not bothered to bind her wrists, for that would take time and Xask believed—quite correctly—that already the Cro-Magnon warriors were in full pursuit. The little man

"There seemed little the savage girl could
do to fight her captors."

wished above all else to put as much distance between himself and the men of Thandar as he could.

But although unbound, it would have been difficult for the Stone Age girl to break free and escape. Fumio kept a tight grasp on her upper arm, yanking her along whenever she pretended to stumble, which she did in order to slow their progress; and, in the thick brush, she could not have gotten far without being caught.

What was needed, Darya perceived, was something in the nature of a timely interruption. Plodding along through the heavy underbrush, the jungle girl resolved to be patient and alert and wait for something to happen.

Because something usually did. . . .

From their vantage high on the ledge, halfway up the mountain, One-Eye and his captive, the unhappy Murg, had watched the battle against the Gorpaks and the victory of the warriors of the two tribes. The Apeman of Kor, like all of his kind, was not extraordinarily intelligent, but he did possess a strong and healthy sense of survival.

Forcing Murg to descend before him—although the scrawny Sotharian squawked and squealed and shuddered from his very first glance into the giddy, vertiginous depths below—One-Eye clambered down the side of the cliff and sought refuge in the jungle. He slew an uld and gnawed hungrily on its raw flesh, not daring to make a fire, as the smoke might give him away to those he deemed his enemies. Murg was too frightened to eat and cowered fearfully, covertly eyeing the huge Neanderthal as he grunted and slobbered over his hasty meal.

If asked, One-Eye could hardly have explained, even to himself, why he had bothered taking the whimpering Sotharian captive. It seemed to be something to do. Perhaps, a bully to his heart's core, the Apeman did not feel quite himself unless he had someone smaller and weaker to push and slap around. At any rate, he was now saddled with the little man, and must put up with his presence. At any time, of course, he could easily have wrung Murg's bony neck and tossed the corpse into a thicket. But, for the time, One-Eye permitted him to live.

Finishing his meal, One-Eye wiped his greasy mouth on his equally greasy hand, kicked Murg to his feet, and plowed off into the jungle. The hulking Drugar had no particular plan in mind; he simply intended to survive. He could have hoped to find his way back to Kor, but the cave kingdom was far away over the misty waters of the Sogar-Jad, and all of the dugout canoes wherewith the Drugars had come to this shore were long since swamped and lost.

One-Eye was a born hunter, and woodcraft was his middle name. He moved through the aisles of the jungle like a huge, shaggy ghost, making little noise. His only desire was to avoid the panjani warriors, and reach the coast of the underground sea. While he cherished notions of revenge against Eric Carstairs, among others, survival was uppermost in his mind.

Quite suddenly, without the slightest warning, the jungle gave way to a smooth, grassy glade. And One-Eye, plunging through the bushes, froze. For he had burst upon an amazing scene—

The timely interruption Darya was waiting for came erelong. The simple philosophy of the jungle girl proved correct and true: here in Zanthodon, things do, indeed, happen.

What happened was that Xask ran into a spiderweb.

In itself, this is neither unusual nor noteworthy. What made this particular web different from the others in Xask's experience was its *size*.

The web stretched like a sticky curtain across the mouth of a jungle aisle. Here, all was dark and dim, for interwoven boughs above blocked the light of day with thick foliage. Thus Xask did not see the spiderweb before running into it, and once he found himself in it, he yielded to amazement.

For the strands which composed the web were of the thickness of his little finger. And the imagination of Xask faltered before picturing the hugeness of the spider that had spun it. . . .

This was exactly the sort of thing Darya had patiently been awaiting. The moment she saw the web she knew exactly what it was. It was the web of a vathrib—an albino spider, swollen to immense size. Such were not uncommonly found in her native country far down the coast of the sea from here.

Caught in the adhesive strands, Xask kicked and struggled, which only served to entangle him more tightly. He shrilled to Fumio for assistance. The big man hesitated, then stepped forward—

Darya kicked his feet out from under him.

As he fell floundering in the bushes, the jungle girl darted away. Snatching the Professor by the arm, propelling him ahead of her, she sprinted across the clearing swift as a gazelle. Then she glided between the close-set boles of two trees, vanishing into the jungle gloom as if the darkness had swallowed her up. The Professor stumbled along, half-blind, through the blackness. Deftly, the Princess of Thandar guided him around obstacles unseen to him.

Behind them, they could hear Fumio cursing wildly as he scrambled to his feet, and the shrill yelps of Xask as he kicked and struggled in the web. Then there came to the ears of the two in their flight a screech of pure terror.

Darya smiled briefly to herself. In her far-off land, the vathrib grow to the size of human infants. That is not very large or intimidating, to be sure: but it is *very* large for a spider. And the vathrib is a ghastly thing to look upon, its swollen belly thick with sickly white fur, exuding a fetid stench, its drooling mandibles clacking greedily, fierce little mad eyes staring, soulless, filled with mindless hunger.

It was the custom of the vathrib of the jungle country down the coast to hide in the leafy boughs above its web until an uld or some other small edible beast blundered into the sticky trap.

Then the oversized albino spider leisurely clambered down its strand to feed.

This must be what had happened in the clearing they left behind them, thought Darya, with cold amusement. And it served Xask and Fumio right!

After a time, she paused to let the old scientist catch his breath, and to orient herself. Darya intended to circle around through the jungle, reentering the encampmnt before the cliffs. As she possessed that uncanny sense of direction which nature has bequeathed to her children in Zanthodon, this did not seem difficult to her.

Alas, it proved more difficult than she had expected. And the reason for this was that when she had plunged into the jungle upon escaping from the clutches of Fumio, she had not taken the time to notice in which direction she was going. Soon she found herself thoroughly lost.

So dense was the jungle at this part of it that Darya could not even estimate her location. She might be fifty yards from the clearing before the cliffs, or half a mile away. The girl strained her ears, but could hear nothing that denoted the presence of men. She did not dare call out, hoping that her voice might reach the ears of the warriors of the two tribes, who were surely searching the woods for her and the old man, since her call might reach other ears. And those other ears might well be those of Xask and Fumio, as for all she knew thay may have somehow survived the attack of the giant spider.

She resolved to go forward warily, tracing a broad, circular route, while employing every keen sense to detect the nearness of men or beasts. If she could hear someone or something as it approached, she and Professor Potter could climb a tree and lie concealed on a branch above the jungle aisles, until the stranger revealed himself as either enemy or friend.

Before long her sensitive ears did indeed detect the approach of an unknown jungle denizen. Perhaps many, for from the amount of noise there seemed to be several of them. She could hear as dry twigs snapped under their feet, as they wnt rustling through the fallen leaves, as they crept through the bushes.

Touching the Professor's arm to get his attention, she pointed to a great tree. Then she sprang up, seized one of the lower boughs, and swung herself into the foliage with the nimble agility of a young acrobat. Eyeing the tree limbs distrustfully, Professor Potter groaned to himself. He ached in every limb and muscle, and even in his hardy youth he had never been very good at climbing trees.

Darya swung down to the sward again to give the old man a boost up. She just boosted him into the tree when three things happened at the same moment.

There burst through the trees almost in front of her a band of swarthy, grinning men brandishing scimitars. Her heart sank, for she recognized them—the Barbary pirates, who had not, after all, given up their search for her. And Achmed ran gloating eyes over her; how pleased would be the *reis* Kâiradine! For Achmed the Moor had watched as Xask and Fumio had carried her and the Professor off, and had followed with all dispatch, eager to seize the jungle girl his captain coveted.

At the identical instant, One-Eye, with Murg cowering in his wake, lurched into the small clearing, saw Darya and lunged for her. Doubtless, it was his intent to seize and silence the two before they had time to utter any outcry which might apprise the pursuing panjani of their presence.

The small, dim eyes of the hulking Neanderthal did not at once notice the Barbary pirates, for his gaze was fixed intently upon the girl alone. But they certainly noticed *him*.

Uttering a startled oath, Achmed sprang forward and lunged with his blade. The point of the scimitar is not a good thrusting weapon; generally, you cut or slice with the edge. But, in a pinch, it can serve.

The steel blade sank into the shaggy breast of One-Eye. Giving voice to a deep-chested, bestial roar, the Neanderthal swung with one huge hand, slapping the Moor aside. Then he lurched back, fumbling with numbed fingers for his stone axe. The blade of the scimitar was still sticking out of his burly chest. Gaze dimming, One-Eye blinked puzzledly down at the glittering thing. He tried to pull it out, but the strength was draining out of his massive arms, and his hands felt cold and lifeless.

His thick, blubbery lips parted, revealing blunt and yellowed tusks. One-Eye tried to say something, but the power of speech had left him. Blood gushed from his open mouth and his one eye glazed, rolling up in his head, revealing the bloodshot white.

Then he toppled over and lay without moving. For a time his huge breast rose and fell as he fought for breath. Then even that motion ceased and he lay still.

Thus perished One-Eye of the Drugars, High Chief of the Apemen of Kor.

And it was upon this astounding scene that Fumio came blundering. He stopped short, turning pale, and did not even try to resist as the corsairs sprang upon him and lashed his wrists behind his back. They bound Darya, too; and then the Barbary pirates led their captives off through the jungle in the direction of the coast and the lagoon, where their longboats still were moored.

As for Murg, no one bothered to notice as he furtively slunk out of sight, concealing himself in the jungle.

And as for the Professor, he clung for dear life to the branch of the tree. Darya had thrust him up just as the Barbary pirates appeared; concealed behind the thick foliage, clinging to the branch with all the strength in his skinny arms and legs, he perforce must watch as the young woman was led off by the corsairs. He was unable to interfere because he was unable to get down.

How could he ever explain his inability to act in Darya's defense to Eric Carstairs—the dear boy—he thought miserably as he hung upside down, waiting for the first monster to come along and have professor for lunch.

Chapter 25.

THE DRAGONMEN OF ZAR

We began to emerge from the cavern city, our tasks there more or less accomplished. As things chanced, Hurok and I were among the first to return out of the hollow mountains. And when we came to the encampment, of course, we discovered everything in a turmoil. Nian and Yualla hastened to apprise us that Xask and Fumio had stolen away Darya and Professor Potter. They did not know either of the two men by name, but I recognized the villains from their descriptions. And my heart sank into my breast.

I felt a little more optimistic as they told me how Ragor, Erdon and seven of the other warriors of Thandar and Sothar had pursued our stolen friends into the jungle. And from that venture they had not as yet returned.

Garth and Tharn and the rest of the tribal warriors had not yet emerged from the cavern city. But I resolved not to waste precious time in delay, and to press on after Darya and her captors myself, with only my small war party. Instructing the folk of the encampment to apprise the two High Chiefs of what had transpired as soon as they reappeared, we caught up our weapons and vanished into the jungles.

With Hurok and Jorn and Varak at my side, I knew that we had little to fear from the likes of Xask and Fumio.

We spread out to comb the jungles, correctly guessing that Xask would have traveled in a straight line, making for the open country. It was Jorn who led the way; the keen eyes of the young huntsman easily followed the trail of the captives and their captors, spotting the imprint of Darya's foot in the loam and even the mark of Fumio's buskins.

"How do you know they belong to Fumio?" I inquired. The blond boy grinned.

"The stitching on the sole is after the fashion of the men

179

of Thandar," he pointed out. "The feet of the men of Sothar
bear stitching after another mode."

We traversed the jungle with all possible speed. Entering a
large glade, we stopped short at the sight of One-Eye's huge,
hairy carcass. I stooped to examine the corpse. He had not
been dead for very long, for the blood upon his breast and
beard was still wet.

"Well, you old rogue," I muttered, half affectionately, "you
finally paid the price for your villainies, didn't you?"

I did not exactly mourn the passing of One-Eye; but somehow life would be a little less livelier here in Zanthodon without him.

Just then a quavering voice came from the treetops.

"I say, my boy, is that you?"

"Doc!" I gasped. "What the hell are you doing up there?"

With dignity he explained shortly that he was simply too
old for these shenanigans. "Your young lady assisted me to
ascend," he said testily. "Once aloft, I found it impossible to
descend again. Then the Barbary pirates appeared, slew that
hulking brute over there, and carried off the young woman
and that rascal Fumio."

I frowned, my face grim. I had a score or two to settle
with Fumio; someday soon, please heaven, we would meet
face to face.

My warriors assisted the Professor out of his tree, and we
continued our search in the direction which he informed us
the pirates had taken. Before very long we came out of the
jungle onto the shore of that little promontory, and there we
found Ragor, Erdon, Warza, Parthon and the other warriors.
They hailed us and we joined them.

"Ragor, have you discovered any sign of the gomad
Darya?" I demanded as we came up to them.

"Alas, Eric Carstairs, they moved too swiftly for us to
overtake them," the warrior said grimly.

I stifled a groan. Then I paused to look around me at the
scene. There, of course, lay the lagoon and the glade and the
river, with the Peaks of Peril beyond. It seemed to me that
this small parcel of real estate had seen a lot more action
than it deserved. In that stream Darya had bathed when first
Redbeard had carried her off; from that copse of trees the
aurochs had charged, scattered Xask, Fumio, One-Eye and
me; there on that stretch of beach Jorn and the Professor had
seen Darya carried aboard the corsair galley; farther up that

curve of sand, Jorn and Darya had waded ashore after escaping from the pirates.

An awful lot had happened in this particular piece of sce-
nery.

Well, the longboats were gone, but we found the place
where they had been concealed. Jorn climbed a tall tree and
reported that he could see the crimson sails of the *Red Witch*
as she sailed farther up along the coast; undoubtedly, my beloved Princess and the villainous Fumio were captives aboard
her.

I resolved in my heart to follow that coast until I discovered the pirate stronghold, and to tear it apart stone by stone,
if necessary, until I rescued my beloved.

For I knew now that it was Darya whom I loved.

I have known many women; I have loved only one.

There came a slight disturbance from our rear. The bushes
crackled, making my warriors spring about, javelins lifted.
But it was only Murg. He was splashed with mud and filthy
from crawling through the bushes, but he seemed unharmed.
Whimpering, he related how he had followed One-Eye and
been captured by him. Then he related an account of Darya's
capture by the corsairs that matched everything Professor
Potter had told us.

I was not particularly pleased to see Murg again, but what
the hell. I had a lot more important things on my mind than
one whining little Sotharian.

"It will take us too long to retrace our way through the
jungle and scale the line of cliffs to the other side," I said to
my warriors. "I mean to pursue the pirate ship to its home
port, wherever in the vastness of Zanthodon that may be."

"And the warriors of Black Hair will accompany him, be it
to the end of life itself," grunted Hurok solemnly. I clapped
him on one huge, ape-like shoulder, not trusting myself to
speak.

"The only thing to do is to circle the promontory, keeping
to the beach," I said. "It's the long way 'round, I suppose, but
it seems the best way to me."

"Eric Carstairs will lead and we, his warriors, will follow,"
vowed Varak of Sothar. I nodded.

"Let's get going," I said shortly.

We trotted up the beach of the lagoon and, to make a long
story short, followed the strand the length of the promontory,
then back along its farther side, which none of us had yet

seen. There was nothing else for Murg to do but trot along unhappily at our rear. I suppose he was reluctant to join in any enterprise so daring and perilous. On the other hand, he didn't care to be left behind all alone. The last time he'd done that sort of thing he had been jumped by One-Eye. One-Eye was dead now, but, for people like Murg, the world is full of One-Eyes.

On the far side of the promontory, the coast stretched away in a long curve. An immense grassy plain met our eyes, larger in its extent than the plain of the trantors on the other side of the Peaks of Peril. Far off beyond the plain, on the misty horizon, we saw dim islands in the sea of Sogar-Jad, and a line of mountains marching down the world. A green mass at the foot of those mountains could only be another sector of jungle country.

"My chieftain, we can make better time by traversing these plains in a straight line than by following the coast of the sea," suggested Jorn diffidently. "See how it curves upon itself."

I agreed instantly. If we crossed the plain in a straight line, we would reach the farther edge of the sea more swiftly than if we followed the meandering curve of the seacoast.

After a very brief rest, we proceeded to do so.

That Xask had survived the attack of the giant spider was due to his own cool nerves. When the shaggy horror had come picking its eight-legged way down the strands of the web, Fumio had turned pale as milk and bolted in pure fear.

I suppose his cowardly reaction was, after all, only natural. Gone was his respect for his divinity: if God cannot get himself out of a spiderweb, what could a mere mortal like Fumio do?

Xask had marshaled his strength and calmed his leaping pulse. Since it did no good to kick and struggle (that only enmeshed him the more tightly in the sticky strands), he would be wiser to apply common sense. Xask lifted his legs off the ground and folded them under him. His weight was slight, for he was a man of slender build, but he still weighed a lot more than the timid little uld for whom the web had been spun.

In a word, the web sagged under the dead weight of the Zarian. The strands stretched; one or two of them snapped. Xask found himself lying on his back upon the sward with only his forearms still caught in the web. Using his feet, he kicked himself backwards until the web stretched even farther. Another strand snapped, then another. Eventually he was free.

During these unexpected actions, the bloated albino spider had prudently ceased its descent. It hung there cautiously watching the strange actions of its prey. When that prey managed to disentangle itself from the web, the spider waited until the man-thing had vanished out of sight, then began patiently and philosophically to repair the damage done to its web.

There will always be another uld, it probably thought to itself.

Xask reached a jungle stream and washed himself, scraping his arms and legs free of the stickiness with handfuls of gritty sand scooped from the bottom. Then he continued on through the jungle with extreme caution.

When he emerged onto the beach, the first thing he saw was Eric Carstairs and his warriors circumambulating the promontory. It was still the desire of the Zarian to capture Eric Carstairs again, so that he could coax or threaten or pry from him the secrets of the thunder-weapon which he still wore at his waist.

So Xask, keeping well out of sight, simply followed our tracks.

When he reached the plain beyond the promontory, our tracks abruptly ceased. It did not take Xask very long to figure out that we were traversing the plain in a straight line in order to save time. It puzzled the clever little Zarian, though. What did we think we were doing? Of course, Xask had no way of knowing about the Princess Darya or the Barbary pirates; but even if he had known, our actions would have remained incomprehensible to him.

For what does a man like Xask know about the love between a man and a woman? All he is capable of feeling is the love of power.

As there was nothing else for him to do, Xask followed us across the plain.

We did not get very far. Intent on running and trying to conserve our strength, we were trotting along, not paying enough attention to the things in our immediate vicinity. This is usually a mistake anywhere; it is a real big mistake to make in Zanthodon. For the Underground World has more surprises than you can imagine.

We ran into a herd of dinosaurs.

They were very big dinosaurs, with long, curving necks and pebbled bronze-and-copper hides.

There were a few things very strange about them. The first thing was that they wore bridles, bits and reins. Another thing that was odd was that they were hunting us.

The third thing was that men were riding on their backs.

"The Dragonmen of Zar!" cried Varak, eyes bulging. "Barely did the warriors of Sothar elude their clutches as we journeyed hither from our lost land! We are doomed, my chieftain!"

By this time the men in the saddles had seen us and were coming about.

"Scatter!" I yelled. "Lose yourselves—hide in the grass!"

Obediently, my men spread out in different directions and hid themselves, even Murg.

It didn't do us much good, though. Leaping from the backs of their gigantic mounts, the Dragonmen pursued. The only ones they caught were the Professor and myself. They prodded us to our feet with slender spears crafted of some light, glittering metal. Then they looked us over, talking among themselves in a tongue I did not recognize but the Professor did. His eyes lit up with that spooky excitement that is the fervor of the scholar.

"By Ventris and Evans!" he breathed, voice quavering. "They are speaking the language of ancient Crete—*Minoan* Crete, by all that's unholy!"

"Yeah?" I said skeptically, while the little men bound my wrists behind me, and others stood guard with leveled spears. "I knew the writings had been deciphered, but I didn't know anybody had figgered out what their lingo sounds like—"

"Well, I have a Theory of my own," he began, eyes glittering. I groaned, having heard *that* one far too many times before.

They dragged us up to share the capacious saddles, tugged the heads of their dragonish steeds around and we went riding off across the plains toward the edge of the distant mountains. My men were widely scattered and had not dared to try to rescue us lest we be slain, I knew.

Suddenly, a small, slim figure that I recognized stepped into our path with lifted arms. The Dragonmen reined their reptiles to a ponderous halt.

"It is Prince Xask!" one of them cried in amazement. "The exile—the outlaw!"

"The Empress has placed him under sentence of death if ever he shows his face among us again," said another. "Let us ride him down—"

"Hold!" cried Xask. "The Sacred Empress will revoke the sentence of death that lies upon my head when she sees the gift I bring to lay at her feet!"

"What gift may that be, Xask the Liar?" demanded the leader, disbelief visible in his countenance.

"The key to the throne of all the world!" cried Xask, taking something from his waist and brandishing it. And my heart sank within me to the chill of a ghastly premonition.

For it was my .45 automatic—the *thunder-weapon*.

The decision was beyond the authority of the captain of this squad of Dragonmen. Binding Xask as we ourselves were bound, he was mounted behind one of the riders, and we continued off lumbering across the plains. Catching my eye, Xask smiled. It wasn't a smile so much as an oily, gloating smirk. I kept my face stony.

We rode away.

But behind us, Hurok the Apeman rose to his feet from the thick grasses where he had concealed himself, and his great hands clenched and unclenched hungrily.

For the only true friend he had in all of Zanthodon had just been carried off into the unknown realm of mystery and marvel—*Zar*.

THE END

But the Adventures of
Eric Carstairs in
the Underground World will continue in
HUROK OF THE STONE AGE
the third volume in this new series.

The *Afterword:*

THE PEOPLE OF ZANTHODON

Editor's Note: At this point, the end of the second volume in this series, it seems to me that the narrative has become so complex that I should supply the reader with a short glossary of the characters thus far introduced into the tale, together with a brief account of their positions in this history.

ACHMED THE MOOR: First mate of the corsair ship *Red Witch*.

BORAG: One of the Drugars on guard at the entrance to Kor when One-Eye returned to the cave country.

BUO: A soldier of the Gorpaks, under the command of Captain Lutho.

COPH: The old wise man of the Sothar tribe; counselor to Garth, the High Chief.

DARYA: Daughter of Tharn and gomad, or Princess, of Thandar. It was Darya who instructed Eric Carstairs in the language of Zanthodon, and with whom he fell in love.

ERDON: A warrior of Thandar.

ERIC CARSTAIRS: The young American soldier of fortune who piloted Professor Potter into Zanthodon; the true author of these adventures.

FATSO: A leader of the Drugar slaves who took Eric and the Professor captive soon after their entry into Zanthodon. "Fatso" was Eric's nickname for this individual; at the time he was still too unfamiliar with the language to catch the name by which his fellow Neanderthals knew him.

FUMIO: One of the chieftains of Thandar, a former suitor for Darya's hand. He betrayed his trust and became an outlaw.

GARTH: High Chief of the Sothar tribe, who made friends

with Eric Carstairs during their period of captivity in the cavern city of the Sluagghs.

GOMAK: One of the Drugars on guard at the entrance to Kor when One-Eye returned with his lone captive, Fumio.

GRONK: Lutho's superior officer in the military hierarchy of the Gorpaks.

HOOM: One of the people of the caverns. Eric Carstairs appointed him leader *pro tem* of his people after their liberation from their Gorpak masters.

HUROK OF KOR: A chieftain and mighty warrior of the Drugars of Kor, who became the friend of Eric Carstairs and his loyal companion on many of his adventures.

ITHAR: A chieftain of the Thandar tribe; leader of the huntsmen who accompanied Tharn on their quest for the solen Darya.

JORN THE HUNTER: The faithful young Cro-Magnon boy who rescued Darya from the embraces of Fumio, and, later, from the arms of Kâiradine Redbeard.

KÂIRADINE REDBEARD: Prince of the Barbary pirates of El-Cazar, and captain of the *Red Witch*. He accounted himself to be the seventh in line of direct succession from the notorious Khair ud-Din of Algiers.

KEMAL THE TURK: A crewman of the *Red Witch*.

KOMAD: Leader of the scouts who accompanied Tharn on the expedition to rescue Darya.

LUTHO: A captain of the Gorpaks.

MURG: A sly and crafty man of the Sothar tribe.

NIAN: The mate of the Omad Garth of Sothar, and mother of Yualla.

NOORKA: A female of the cavern folk.

ONE-EYE: A chieftain of the Drugars of Kor; upon the death of Uruk he seized the role of High Chief, but never really ruled.

OTHA: The chef of the Gorpak kitchens.

PARTHON: A Sotharian warrior.

THE PROFESSOR: Professor Percival P. Potter, Ph.D., scientist, savant, explorer and all-around polymath.

QUEB: Witch doctor of the Gorpaks and priest of the Sluaggh cult.

RAGOR: One of the warriors of Thandar.

RUKH: A chieftain of the Sothar tribe, imprisoned with Eric and the others in the cavern city.

SUNTH: One of the Gorpak soldiers.

TARBU: A Barbary pirate.

THARN OF THANDAR: High Chief of his tribe; Darya's mighty sire and Eric Carstairs' loyal friend.

THUSK: One of the men of Sothar. Eric was never quite certain that he correctly remembered the name of this man.

UNGG: One of the Gorpaks of the cavern city.

URUK: High Chief of Kor, and a dreadful ogre of incredible ugliness and bestial cruelty. Eric put a bullet through his brain just before the stampeding thantors crushed the Drugar host.

VARAK: A fine young warrior of Sothar who became one of Eric's friends.

VUSK: A Gorpak soldier under Lutho's command.

WARZA: One of the warriors of Thandar.

XASK: A strange personage of mysterious origin; exiled from the Scarlet City of Zar, he became vizier to Uruk of Kor. Much of the mystery surrounding him will be explained in the third volume of these narratives.

YUALLA: A Sotharian maid; the teen-aged daughter of Garth the High Chief of that tribe.

ZORAIDA: A dancing-girl of El-Cazar. Of Moorish descent, like Achmed, she was his rival in influence over Kâiradine Redbeard.

and

"THE EMPRESS": An unknown woman, presumably the sovereign of the Scarlet City. Very much concerning her will be explained in the third book of this series.

Presenting MICHAEL MOORCOCK
in DAW editions

The Elric Novels

- [ ] ELRIC OF MELNIBONE (#UW1356—$1.50)
- [ ] THE SAILOR ON THE SEAS OF FATE (#UW1434—$1.50)
- [ ] THE WEIRD OF THE WHITE WOLF (#UE1528—$1.75)
- [ ] THE VANISHING TOWER (#UE1553—$1.75)
- [ ] THE BANE OF THE BLACK SWORD (#UE1515—$1.75)
- [ ] STORMBRINGER (#UE1574—$1.75)

The Runestaff Novels

- [ ] THE JEWEL IN THE SKULL (#UE1547—$1.75)
- [ ] THE MAD GOD'S AMULET (#UW1391—$1.50)
- [ ] THE SWORD OF THE DAWN (#UW1392—$1.50)
- [ ] THE RUNESTAFF (#UW1422—$1.50)

The Michael Kane Novels

- [ ] CITY OF THE BEAST (#UW1436—$1.50)
- [ ] LORD OF THE SPIDERS (#UW1443—$1.50)
- [ ] MASTERS OF THE PIT (#UW1450—$1.50)

The Oswald Bastable Novels

- [ ] THE WARLORD OF THE AIR (#UW1380—$1.50)
- [ ] THE LAND LEVIATHAN (#UW1448—$1.50)

Other Titles

- [ ] LEGENDS FROM THE END OF TIME (#UY1281—$1.25)
- [ ] A MESSIAH AT THE END OF TIME (#UW1358—$1.50)
- [ ] DYING FOR TOMORROW (#UW1366—$1.50)
- [ ] THE RITUALS OF INFINITY (#UW1404—$1.50)
- [ ] THE TIME DWELLER (#UE1489—$1.75)

If you wish to order these titles,

please see the coupon in

the back of this book.

Attention:

DAW COLLECTORS

Many readers of DAW Books have written requesting information on early titles and book numbers to assist in the collection of DAW editions since the first of our titles appeared in April 1972.

We have prepared a several-pages-long list of all DAW titles, giving their sequence numbers, original and current order numbers, and ISBN numbers. And of course the authors and book titles, as well as reissues.

If you think that this list will be of help, you may have a copy by writing to the address below and enclosing fifty cents in stamps or coins to cover the handling and postage costs.

DAW BOOKS, INC. Dept. C
1633 Broadway
New York, N.Y. 10019

DRAY PRESCOT

The great novels of Kregen, world of Antares

- [ ] **TRANSIT TO SCORPIO**   (#UY1169—$1.25)
- [ ] **WARRIOR OF SCORPIO**   (#UY1212—$1.25)
- [ ] **SWORDSHIPS OF SCORPIO**   (#UY1231—$1.25)
- [ ] **PRINCE OF SCORPIO**   (#UY1251—$1.25)
- [ ] **ARMADA OF ANTARES**   (#UY1227—$1.25)
- [ ] **KROZAIR OF KREGEN**   (#UW1288—$1.50)
- [ ] **SECRET SCORPIO**   (#UW1344—$1.50)
- [ ] **SAVAGE SCORPIO**   (#UW1372—$1.50)
- [ ] **CAPTIVE SCORPIO**   (#UW1394—$1.50)
- [ ] **GOLDEN SCORPIO**   (#UW1424—$1.50)
- [ ] **A LIFE FOR KREGEN**   (#UE1456—$1.75)
- [ ] **A SWORD FOR KREGEN**   (#UJ1485—$1.95)
- [ ] **A FORTUNE FOR KREGEN**   (#UJ1505—$1.95)
- [ ] **A VICTORY FOR KREGEN**   (#UJ1532—$1.95)

Fully illustrated

If you wish to order these titles,

please use the coupon on

the last page of this book.

DAW BOOKS presents ...

LIN CARTER

The Green Star series

- [ ] **UNDER THE GREEN STAR** (#UW1433—$1.50)
- [ ] **WHEN THE GREEN STAR CALLS** (#UY1267—$1.25)
- [ ] **BY THE LIGHT OF THE GREEN STAR** (#UY1268—$1.25)
- [ ] **AS THE GREEN STAR RISES** (#UY1156—$1.25)
- [ ] **IN THE GREEN STAR'S GLOW** (#UY1399—$1.25)

The Gondwane series

- [ ] **THE WARRIOR OF WORLD'S END** (#UW1420—$1.50)
- [ ] **THE ENCHANTRESS OF WORLD'S END** (#UY1172—$1.25)
- [ ] **THE IMMORTAL OF WORLD'S END** (#UY1254—$1.25)
- [ ] **THE BARBARIAN OF WORLD'S END** (#UW1300—$1.50)
- [ ] **THE PIRATE OF WORLD'S END** (#UE1410—$1.75)

Plus

- [ ] **THE WIZARD OF ZAO** (#UE1383—$1.75)
- [ ] **JOURNEY TO THE UNDERGROUND WORLD**
  (#UE1499—$1.75)

DAW BOOKS are represented by the publishers of Signet and Mentor Books, THE NEW AMERICAN LIBRARY, INC.

THE NEW AMERICAN LIBRARY, INC.,
P.O. Box 999, Bergenfield, New Jersey 07621

Please send me the DAW BOOKS I have checked above. I am enclosing
$_____ (check or money order—no currency or C.O.D.'s).
Please include the list price plus 50¢ per order to cover handling costs.

Name _____

Address _____

City _____ State _____ Zip Code _____

Please allow at least 4 weeks for delivery